# The worl
## enough of

"A **most beguiling protagonist!**"
*New York Times*

"Miss Seeton gets into wild drama with fine touches
of farce ... This is a **lovely mixture of the funny and
the exciting.**"
*San Francisco Chronicle*

"This is not so much black comedy as black-currant
comedy ... **You can't stop reading. Or laughing.**"
*The Sun*

"**Depth of description and lively characters** bring this
English village to life."
*Publishers Weekly*

"Fun to be had with a **full cast of endearingly zany
villagers** ... and the ever gently intuitive Miss Seeton."
*Kirkus Reviews*

"Miss Seeton is the **most delightfully satisfactory character
since Miss Marple.**"
Ogden Nash

"**She's a joy!**"
*Cleveland Plain Dealer*

# Picture Miss Seeton

## A MISS SEETON MYSTERY

### Heron Carvic

This edition published in 2017 by Farrago, an imprint of
Prelude Books Ltd
13 Carrington Road, Richmond, TW10 5AA, United Kingdom

www.farragobooks.com

First published by Geoffrey Bles in 1968

ISBN: 978-1-911440-53-6

# Have you read them all?

Treat yourself again to the first Miss Seeton novels—

### Picture Miss Seeton
A night at the opera strikes a chord of danger when
Miss Seeton witnesses a murder ... and paints a portrait
of the killer.

### Miss Seeton Draws the Line
Miss Seeton is enlisted by Scotland Yard when her paintings
of a little girl turn the young subject into a model for murder.

### Witch Miss Seeton
Double, double, toil and trouble sweep through the village
when Miss Seeton goes undercover ... to investigate a local
witches' coven!

---

Turn to the end of this book for a full list of the series,
plus—on the last page—**exclusive access to
the Miss Seeton short story** that started it all.

# Chapter 1

"L'*amour* est *tum* tum
    *De* some*thing* ..."
So colorful. Not romantic—no, one couldn't call it that;
if anything perhaps a trifle sordid. Carmen, herself, for
instance, no better than she should be. In fact, if one were
frank, worse. And the other girl, the young one; it was difficult to feel sorry for her. Her fiancé, quite obsessed with
his mother—obviously weak and easily influenced—would
have made a most unsatisfactory husband in any case. Still,
for him to stab Carmen at the end like that—so unnecessary.
Almost contrived. Though, of course, one must not forget
that foreigners felt differently about these matters. One read
that people abroad did frequently get emotional and kill each
other. Probably the heat.

Miss Seeton stepped aside to avoid a pile of crates. She
peered at them.

Seville oranges. How interesting. Spain. Such an odd
coincidence. One might almost think that one was back in
one's seat at the theatre, with the warm glow of the lights.

"Qui n'a ja*mais*, ja*mais*
    Tum *tum* some*thing*."

Cracked, yes. Off-key, yes, but a warm glow had started up inside Miss Seeton. Her visit to the opera tonight was really in the nature of a celebration. Tomorrow morning she would set out on an adventure. No—no, that was putting it too strongly. Set out upon a new way of life—or at least the beginning of a new way. Which would be, of course, in its way, an adventure. For her.

Where was she now? If she turned right here—gracious, how dark this alleyway looked. Should people park their cars all down one side? With their wheels on the pavement too?—it should take her towards Tottenham Court Road. Or she might even catch her bus in Charing Cross Road.

This walk had been a good idea. She felt quite a spring in her step. Was it her rubber soles? Or could it be—could it be just possibly that THEY were doing her good. Miss Seeton drew in her breath; braced herself. Of course it was ridiculous taking up exercises at her age—but that advertisement had looked so encouraging. Even when the book arrived and one realised the difficulties, it had still appeared to be worth trying. There was no question the tiresome stiffness in her knees did seem to be better. A lot of the positions were—well, embarrassing. Even to oneself. But, after all, if no one knew—and if it helped. Oh …

Miss Seeton prepared to hurry by a couple pressed into an adjacent doorway, when the girl spat:

"Merdes-toi, putain. Saligaud! Scélérat, si tu m'muertes …" She ended on a gasp as the boy's arm drove into her side.

Oh, no. Really. Miss Seeton stopped. Even supposing the girl had been rude—and it had certainly sounded so—that

2

was no excuse. A gentleman did not hit … She prodded him in the back with her umbrella.

"Young man …"

He whirled and leaped. Deflected by the umbrella, he landed beside the prostrate Miss Seeton. Grabbing her by the coat, he jerked her towards him. A blaze of light froze him as the head-lights of a car farther down the alley were switched on and an engine started. There was a scuffle of movement and, her coat released, Miss Seeton fell back on her elbows as the boy jumped to his feet and ran. With the help of her umbrella she pushed herself upright. Really! The foreign temperament—so impulsive.

A car door slammed. A man's voice called, "Stay where you are, Mabel." The thwack of running footsteps.

"Are you all right, madam? What happened?"

Miss Seeton looked around. A heavy middle-aged man appeared from behind the beam of light, hurried towards her and grasped her arm.

"That man who attacked you—did he hurt you?"

Miss Seeton, a little breathless, considered. "No—no, I don't think so. It was just the surprise."

"But you were on the ground," the man insisted. "He had hold of you."

"It was all so unexpected. I startled him, you see, and it made him jump. We both fell down. Then he pulled me. I think he was trying to help me up."

"Then why did he run?"

She appeared puzzled. "Well, there was the girl—such bad manners. But then, of course, he's not English."

"The girl? What girl?"

"They were in that doorway there. She cried out something that sounded rude and he hit her. I'm afraid I interfered. I do

3

think, don't you," she continued earnestly, "that the young must learn to behave. Surely? Even abroad?"

The man glanced at the empty doorway, took a step and, leaning on the bonnet of one of the parked cars, saw the huddled body of a girl wedged between the wing of the car and the wall.

"Good God—you're right! He knocked her out. Just a minute, I'll prop her up against the door."

Miss Seeton moved to help. "Perhaps she's fainted, poor thing. Oh …" She gave a shocked cry. As the man shifted the body the girl's coat fell back and the glare of the headlamp shone on the handle of the knife in her side. "No, wait. Don't move her yet. We must get a doctor. She—look, she's been stabbed."

Stabbed. But of course. Stabbed. That was inevitable somehow. This dazzlement of light—spotlights. The slope of the alley steepened. To keep her balance Miss Seeton leaned against the car. Spotlights. Oranges. Seville. That was it. It had happened before. She'd seen it—watched it happen before.

Someone was speaking to her, urgently. "It's too late for a doctor. This girl is dead. We must get the police." The man gazed almost in awe at the little figure, hat askew, coat awry, gloved hands still clasping her umbrella. "You mean you actually saw this happen? What made him do it?"

Miss Seeton straightened. "He has to," she explained. "It's the last act." She shook her head. Suddenly she felt very tired. "But it's so silly really. And quite—it's quite unnecessary."


"Would you like another cup of tea, miss?" The constable at Bow Street Police Station made the suggestion as a conversational gambit to break an awkward silence.

Miss Seeton contemplated the emulsive remains of what appeared to be sweetened tar at the bottom of her cup. "How kind." Although the room was warm it was true she felt a little cold. "If I might have it very weak—nearly all water—and with no sugar, I should be most grateful."

"Sure you won't have something to eat while you're waiting?"

"No, really, I had a meal before the theatre. But—" She hesitated. "I wonder if you'd be kind enough to ask about my handbag. I'm a little worried; you see, it's getting late and I have no money on me—also there's my latchkey."

The constable turned at the door. "Don't you worry about that, miss. We'll see you get home all right. And, as for your bag, the boys have got a description; if it's there they'll find it and let you know at once. Anyway, it won't be long now, the Yard should be here any minute. I'll go and rustle up your tea." He closed the door behind him with a sigh of relief. Funny little old trout. You'd think she'd be all of a twit, but she was as calm as you please. Probably came of teaching kids. Once you'd coped with kids these days you'd copped the lot.

Miss Seeton looked up as the door opened. A grey day on heathland came in briskly, followed by a footballer. No—really, this was too fanciful; she must be tired, next she would be seeing people as shapes with holes in them. A perfectly ordinary, tall, rugged, middle-aged man in tweeds, followed by a perfectly ordinary, though very large, scrubbed young man in a dark suit. It made no difference. She was still left with the impression of a grey sky and heather ruffled in the wind. And the young man's suit was entirely wasted. He might just as well have been wearing  in fact more appropriately—several yards of striped wool muffler, shorts and those stockings one associated with *Alice in Wonderland*; except, of course, that footballers' stockings were shorter and thicker.

The grey day—the older man smiled and spoke:

"Miss Seeton? No, please don't get up. I'm Superintendent Delphick of Scotland Yard and this is Detective-Sergeant Ranger from the same locality." He moved to behind the desk and sat down. The sergeant settled on an unobtrusive chair to one side. "Very good of you to agree to wait for us. Sorry if we've been rather long, but we both had to be dug out of our respective homes as we were not on duty."

"I'm so sorry." Miss Seeton looked distressed. "I'm afraid it was my fault …"

The superintendent raised an eyebrow. "Hardly yours, Miss Seeton. Quite the reverse in fact. They sent for us because there may be a tie-up with another case of mine, so it was thought better we should be in on it from the start. We knew the girl, you see."

"That poor girl who was killed."

"Not so poor as all that." His tone was dry. "She was a known prostitute."

"Oh, dear," Miss Seeton exclaimed. "A very hard life; such late hours—and then, of course, the weather. And so unrewarding one would imagine."

"Not necessarily. Like every other walk in life it depends on how far you rise in your profession."

Sergeant Ranger nearly dropped his pen. The Oracle was going it a bit, wasn't he? You didn't come straight out with words like prostitute and then a discussion on fees to somebody like this Miss Seeton. You wrapped it up. He tried wrapping it up. She was an—er—prostitute. The 'er' didn't really make it any better and 'um' actually made it worse. Perhaps The Oracle was right. Anyway the old girl hadn't turned a hair.

"I wouldn't waste too much sympathy on her," Superintendent Delphick continued. "She was a vicious little piece from all accounts. Yes?" in answer to a knock on the door.

The constable came in balancing a cup and saucer. "The lady's tea, sir." He put it on the desk beside her.

The sergeant was moved to protest. "Good Lord, what's that? Drain water?"

"Very weak, as requested. No sugar," he announced.

"Thank you," said Miss Seeton. "You see I don't really care for …"

"Burnt molasses any more than I do," agreed the superintendent. "You might bring me a cup of the same, if you can manage it, and some stewed treacle for the sergeant."

"Right away, sir." The constable left.

Miss Seeton sipped. Much better. Rather comforting.

"Now," he picked up a sheet of paper from the desk and scanned it as he spoke, "in your statement, you say that your assailant was a foreigner. Is that right?" The sergeant looked up from his notes. Now they were getting some place. He underlined the symbol for foreigner. "You don't know his nationality, merely that he was definitely not English." Miss Seeton nodded. "Now, can you make any guess—from anything he said, for instance?"

"No …" She thought. "… No. You see, he never spoke." She ended on a note of faint surprise.

"But you still maintain he was not English. What makes you so certain of that? No, no," he added hastily, as he saw

7

her troubled expression, "I'm not doubting your conclusions. What I want to get at are your reasons for drawing those conclusions. To put myself, as far as possible, in your place. To see and feel what you saw and felt at the time."

Miss Seeton's face cleared. "Well, it was really the girl, you see. She spoke to him—or rather snapped at him in what sounded like French, though I can't be sure. I didn't recognise the actual words but, of course, she was speaking quickly and my French isn't very good. And then he hit her—or that's what it looked like at the time. You see, if he'd been English, he wouldn't have understood her, would he?"

The sergeant studied his underlined 'foreigner'. He added a question mark. He added two more. They didn't express his feelings. He added three exclamation marks and felt better.

"You're probably right," the superintendent agreed. "The girl, though she could speak English, was in fact French by birth. So if you heard her speaking in French, the likelihood is that any previous conversation was in the same language."

The sergeant surreptitiously crossed out all but the smallest of the queries after 'foreigner'.

"You also say," Superintendent Delphick went on, "that you can't give an exact description of the man, though you would recognise him again if you saw him. Is that correct?"

"Well, yes. It's difficult," Miss Seeton explained, "it was all so quick—and rather dark. And then, of course, I wasn't expecting … All I remember is long hair and his expression. An impression really."

Sergeant Ranger regarded his pothooks. That should help. An all-stations call for a long-haired expression should get them places. But fast.

8

"An impression—quite." The superintendent smiled. "Doubt anyone could do better in the circumstances. What I'm getting at is that that impression is photographed in your mind; and we've got to try and find some means of developing the photograph for our own use. I see from this," he tapped the paper, "that you teach drawing."

"But only at a very small school," she affirmed. "In Hampstead. And not on the regular staff; merely attached. I also teach at the Polytechnic—night classes, you know. And a few private pupils that I ..." Her voice trailed off, "I'm so sorry. I'm wandering from the point."

"But you're not. That is the point. The point being that you are an artist. What I want you to do if you will," he leaned across the desk, "is to take this paper and pencil, sit quietly, concentrate on that impression in your mind, then see if you can get it down on paper. Don't worry if you can't. It's just a shot in the dark that might possibly come off. Take your time. It'll give me a chance to catch up on these statements. Come in," he called as he gathered up the papers and settled back in his chair.

The constable entered with a tray and placed two cups of tea on the desk. "One strong with, one weak without, sir." The superintendent nodded and the constable departed.

A shot in the dark. In the dark. Miss Seeton closed her eyes and concentrated. In the dark ...

The superintendent skimmed through the longest of the statements. "Mrs. Mabel Dorothea Walters, 14 Lime Avenue, Barnet, Herts. 'I have never been so shocked ... da-da ... My nerves ... di-da ... I was shattered ... di-da ... In all my life ... di-di-da ... I really feel I must ... di-da-diddy.'" Useless, except to the woman's psychiatrist. He added a footnote: Stayed in car. Saw nothing. Suggest not called inquest. See coroner. He started on the next: "Edward Cyril Walters, 14 Lime etc … On leaving the Cambridge Theatre etc … switched on lights and engine … figures on ground … he ran … I ran … I found … I tried … she said … I said … She said 'He had to do it.' And something about it being his last act 'but not necessary'." He frowned and ringed the last two sentences. He made another note: Straightforward, factual, but saw nothing. Useless, except as confirmation of witness Seeton.

Sergeant Ranger drank his tea. H'm, not bad. At least it had some taste. Better than that hog-wash the super went for. What did The Oracle think he was doing, sitting there browsing over all that bumph. At this rate they'd be at it all night and no forrader. He ought to be questioning the old girl; force a description out of her, not start art classes. Anyway, she'd gone to sleep. Tired, poor old thing, and no wonder. But it was no good them both sitting on their fannies while she had a kip. He got up and took his empty cup to a desk against the wall. Coming back, he stopped behind Miss Seeton and looked over her shoulder.

In the dark …

Be damned—she was having a go. No, she wasn't, she was doodling. Just some straight lines … and then a lot more lines scrubbed in, in a sort of mess. He looked up and caught the superintendent's eye fixed on him, daring him to move— almost to breathe.

In the dark …

Stripes … Hell, no, they weren't, they were bars. An eye … two eyes, staring among all those lines. No, he could see now: two eyes glaring in the dark. But, why behind bars?

What were those squiggles? … Hair—long hair … "Good God!" he exploded. "Caesar!"

Miss Seeton jumped. "Oh, no. More hair—and then, of course, no wreath."

The superintendent caught the drawing as it fell, glanced at it, pushed the telephone towards the sergeant: "Check that we've got Lebel's photograph on file," turned back. "Nice work." He beamed at her. "I had a feeling you'd come up with it. Nice work, indeed. Saves a lot of fuss and fluster."

She looked pleased. "You do recognize him, then?"

"Yes, unquestionably César Lebel. Tell me," he studied the drawing, "why the bars?"

"Oh, dear." She bit her lip. "I'm so sorry, that was quite unintentional. It is the sort of thing I'm always trying to stop. In my pupils, I mean—and, naturally, in myself. I do maintain one should draw only what is there; particularly when you're learning—and so it must apply to teaching too. Until you have learnt. And then, of course, it doesn't matter, does it? I mean it's always permissible to break a rule, provided one understands what that rule is. But I do find it difficult at times to differentiate between what is really there and what one thinks one sees. Especially when working from memory. Somehow"—she hesitated—"I seem to remember that young man as a—a caged animal."

"You're dead on. Has been, and will be again. A violent tyke. English born, French parents. In trouble on and off since a kid."

"They've got mug shots, sir," the sergeant broke in. "Do you want to speak?"

"Yes." He took the phone. "Harry? … Good. Run some prints and to save me time get them to put out an

11

all-stations for him, would you? … No, not the 'Help with inquiries' lark. 'Wanted in connection with the murder of Mrs. Hickson; born Marie Prévost' and see the Press get it … I know, but I want to give the impression the case is sewn up … No, no dabs, not a damn thing except one eye-witness ident … Exactly, that's the danger. I want Lebel and his lot to think there's more. That we've got him cold … Thanks. Be seeing you." He cradled the receiver and turned back. "Now, Miss Seeton, can you bear with us a little longer, or would you rather we finished this in the morning?"

"I think now would be best. That is if you don't mind and if it won't keep you too late. You see," she apologised, "I have to set out early in the morning for the country. Also I don't think they've found my bag yet. They promised to let me know because without my latchkey I can't get in. My spare key is in my desk."

"Your handbag, yes." He regarded her seriously. "I wanted to talk to you about that. It's not at the scene of the crime and, I should say, almost certainly stolen."

"Stolen? But there was no one there. Only that nice Mr. Walters, so kind and helpful. He would never …"

"No, not Mr. Walters. Young César."

"But—but he hadn't time."

"Not when you were on the ground?"

Miss Seeton gave it thought. "Well—yes, I suppose it is just possible."

"Probable, I'm afraid. That is the main reason you were asked to stay on here. From your description of the contents," he referred to the papers, "some silver in purse, two pound notes …"

"Just for emergencies," she explained. "I don't keep more in my bag than I need because you never know, do you? And then, of course, at school—such a temptation. So unfair I always think."

"Very sensible," he agreed. "Now, let's see—handkerchief, comb, mirror, key to flat … ah, yes, here we are, diary containing name and address. The local police have been contacted and a watch is being kept on the house."

"A watch? But I don't understand."

"Don't you realise you could be in danger yourself? Lebel might very well make an attempt to kill you."

"Me?" Miss Seeton expostulated. "But that's ridiculous. I don't even know him."

"I doubt he's a stickler for the social conventions," the superintendent remarked. "If he thinks you're the only witness that can identify him, his best bet is to eliminate you. I'd like to suggest we arrange accommodation for you at an hotel for the night."

She became flustered. "I'm sorry, that would really be rather inconvenient. I—I've nothing with me. And then I still have some packing to do."

"Very well. In that case, with your permission, we'll have a policewoman spend the rest of the night with you. She can see you off in the morning. Meanwhile may we clear up one or two points in your statement. You say 'He had his back to me. Then he hit the girl. I spoke to him. Then he turned round and jumped and we both fell down.' I can't think why he jumped you—why didn't he just make a run for it? If he hadn't turned round you would never have seen his face at all."

"That was my fault, I'm afraid. I interrupted him and that rather took him aback, I think."

In defiance of control the superintendent's lip twitched. "I can see it would," he acknowledged.

"Actually—" Oh, dear, this was most embarrasing. It sounded so—so aggressive. But she must be exact. "Actually I was a little angry—at his rudeness, you know—so I poked him in the back with my umbrella. It was that that made him jump."

Holy cow! The sergeant's pen clattered on the floor. Only rigid training stopped him throwing his notebook after it. Go on, give her the George Medal and be done with it. Give her the bar as well. Give her the commissioner's job and let 'em all go home. Strong men thought twice about tackling young Caesar in a temper. But not this little hen. Oh, no. Stick him in the back with a brolly, right in the middle of a murder and tell him to stop it at once. A few more like her and crime would be all washed up and they could concentrate on traffic offences like the public thought they did.

"When you're ready, Sergeant."

The young man, red-faced under the stem gaze of his superior, retrieved his pen and straightened. "Yes, sir. Sorry, sir." How did The Oracle remain cool as a cold-blooded cucumber? Even a bit grim. Though, come to think of it, pinker than usual and sort of quivering at the edges.

"Thank you, Miss Seeton." The superintendent's voice was grave. "I have a very clear picture of events now." He had, too. Took him aback! He betted it had. Took him right back to his cradle, he shouldn't wonder. It was a delightful thought—but, no, not for now. For reflection later—preferably when he was alone. He set his jaw and conjured up serious thoughts. Car smashes. Murders—no, not murders—not just at the moment. Fire, famine and flood. "There is one other thing," he continued, "it's in Mr. Walters's statement. With reference to Lebel, Mr. Walters quotes you as having said: 'He had to do it'—and something about it's being his last act, but not necessary. Can you remember what you meant by that?"

The sergeant shied. Oh, no, not again.

"But that was nothing to do with him," she pointed out, "that was the other one."

"Other one?" Delphick was sharp. Both detectives stiffened like pointers.

"Don José, in the last act," she explained.

"Ah," the superintendent relaxed. He leafed through the papers. "The beginning of your statement reads 'I was proceeding along Long Acre …' You had, in fact, come from Covent Garden. From *Carmen*?"

"Yes, of course."

"Of course," he agreed, "and I'm bound to admit I'm with you about his stabbing her—quite unnecessary. If he had to behave so stupidly in the first place, he'd have done far better at the end to mind his own business and stab himself. More sensible but less dramatic."

Sergeant Ranger re-read his last notes. He had an uncomfortable feeling of weightlessness. Cloud-cuckoo-land? Or Outer Space.

The superintendent pulled forward a memo-pad. "May I have your address in the country, in case I need to get in touch with you before the inquest?"

"The inquest?" For a moment she was at a loss. "I hadn't realised … I suppose I have to attend that."

"Unavoidable, I'm afraid. At least it should be short and straightforward. Did you intend to be away long?"

"About three weeks. I've got a little cottage in the country. The address is 'Sweetbriars, Plummergen, Kent'."

"There was no note of this address in your handbag, by any chance, was there?" Delphick asked quickly.

"No, I hadn't put it in my diary yet. It would have been so final, somehow. You see, I hardly feel it belongs to me. Or rather it does, of course—but only just. My godmother, who was a cousin of my mother's, died recently and left it to me—she'd lived there most of her life. Also a little money, which makes it possible. I've been down once or twice to arrange things, but not to stay. I'd been thinking of retiring next year—though it's always so difficult to know what to do for the best and, then again, whether one can manage. It was like an answer, really. As my holidays started today, I thought I'd spend the time there, to see how I get on. With the idea of living there permanently, eventually. If it works, that is."

"Are you on the phone there?"

"Yes, Plummergen 35. Luckily my godmother had had it installed—though latterly she used it very little, I think. She was ninety-eight when she died and rather deaf."

He stood up. "Well, thank you, Miss Seeton. I mean that sincerely. You've given us more help than I could have believed possible. Certainly a great deal more than we had any right to expect." She rose and began to pull on her gloves. "I'll see that you're notified about the inquest and we shall meet there. I hope, for your sake, that we don't have to disturb you before. Though if we're lucky enough to lay our hands on Lebel, we might have to call on you for identification. It would depend what sort of story he cooked up. Meanwhile I hope you can put the whole unpleasant experience out of your mind and enjoy the Vale of Kent." He shook hands with her. "The sergeant will take you down and arrange for a policewoman to accompany you. The car's already waiting."

Miss Seeton moved hesitantly to the door; she appeared abstracted. Sergeant Ranger collected her umbrella, towered over her and bowed. "Your small arms, ma'am."

She thanked him with a vague smile and looked past him to the superintendent. "You've been very kind. I'm sorry to seem insistent, but it's my key …"

"Not to worry." He grinned at her. "I think you'll find that, one way or another, the police will discover a means of opening your door. Though I'd feel happier if, before you leave in the morning, you'd arrange to have your lock changed."

He watched as the sergeant led her out and closed the door behind them. Comic little cuss. She'd be all right tonight with a policewoman there and the locals alerted, but he had a nasty feeling that when she'd stuck her brolly into César Lebel, she'd stuck it into a hornet's nest.

# Chapter 2

Miss Seeton waved; the platform at Charing Cross began to move past her, she settled back in her seat. What a charming girl; and the uniform, neat and becoming. How did she manage to look so fresh after sitting in a chair all night? What a tiring life it must be. She'd offered to let down the Put-U-Up, but no, the girl wouldn't have it; she preferred to sit and read. How clever the police were altogether; and what a lot they seemed to know. She'd been really worried about how to get into the flat, but one of them had just sort of fiddled with the lock and the door had opened straight away. It would happen that that inquisitive Mrs. Perrsons from below—a most unsuitable dressing-gown—should choose just that moment to come up and ask "Are you in trouble, dear?" How could she be in trouble when she was surrounded by police? Well, she hadn't been surrounded exactly; there were only two of them besides the girl; but it had seemed rather a crowd in a small flat; examining everything and asking her to see if anything was out of place. Thank goodness, nothing was. Except, perhaps, the kitchen window, which wasn't of course out of place, merely open. Surely she'd not forgotten to shut that? She couldn't remember forgetting it. Anyhow it had obviously interested them and they had insisted on dusting it for fingerprints, though you could hardly call it dusting when it meant blowing powder over everything and making rather a mess. One of them had even got out on the fire-escape and powdered out there, too. However, apparently there weren't any fingerprints, not even her own; it was what they called 'wiped clean' which sounded most satisfactory; she must have forgotten it after all.

This morning had been dreadful. The bell ringing the whole time, or else the telephone, or both together. So distracting when one was trying to remember if one had packed everything one needed. And that interfering Mrs. Perrsons coming up again, offering to help—when all was said, she hardly knew the woman—and asking endless silly questions. She wondered how she would have managed without that police-girl, calm and efficient, arranging to have the lock changed, ordering a taxi and then getting them into it, with the help of the policeman outside, through that crowd on the pavement—newspaper reporters, apparently—you'd have thought they had more important things to do. Why should they want flashlights for taking photographs in daylight?

Nevertheless they'd got away and here she was. She couldn't help feeling excited. It was exciting setting out for one's own place in the country. One's own. Well, she hoped it would become her own. Home. The country. Miss Seeton looked out of the window at the endless vista of streets and buildings. Not quite yet of course. She picked up *The Times*. "Prime Minister Flies to New York." "The Moon Next Year?" "Road Deaths Up Again!" "Murder in Covent Garden." She opened the paper. Ah, now this was interesting. "How Does Your Garden Grow?" How indeed?

That was what she must learn. "A simple, easy way ... nitrogen ... mulch ... phosphates ..." Oh dear, it sounded extremely complicated. Still, she had bought that book *Greenfinger Points the Way* and she'd be able to look it all up in that when she arrived.

Tradition makes Brettenden the accepted station for Plummergen. It is also the main shopping centre. Although a little farther than Rye, it is the inevitable choice since it satisfies that basic requirement of all English travellers that the end should resemble, as nearly as possible, the beginning of their journey. Brettenden is, in essence, an enlarged version of Plummergen.

The town of Brettenden consists virtually of one main artery, the High Street, a wide avenue stretching over a mile from East Cross to West Cross, tree-lined for half its length and ranged with shops on either side. There are innumerable lanes and byways, but as these are, for the most part, shopless they are of little interest to visitors. At East Cross the High Street splits, the left fork becoming Virgin's Lane, which, after two slow curves, turns sharp left round a public house and sweeps up a long hill to the end of the town. Virgin's Lane, though a wide road and bounded by more shops that houses, is not regarded as part of Brettenden proper and the district is, in fact, subtitled Les Marys.

The right, and residential, fork at East Cross is labelled Plummergen Road—the Plummergen end is labelled Brettenden Road. This, though it leaves some doubt as to the road's official designation, leaves travellers from either direction in no doubt as to their destination. Despite the fact that it is necessary to visit the emporiums in Brettenden for many essentials, Plummergen itself is not ill-served in respect of shops.

The street, or more properly, The Street—Plummergen has only the one and admits it—is straight, wide and tree-lined, a quarter of a mile long, hedged on both sides by a medley of houses, cottages and shops in a variety of styles ranging over some four hundred years, two public houses, one blacksmith, the police station and a garage. It is not beautiful, but it has charm; it had also, on the last count, five hundred and one inhabitants.

Apart from the tiny, bow-fronted bakery—sweets, tobacco, cakes and bread, the latter no longer home-made since it has become no more than an outpost of Winesart's empire, which supplies most of Kent and Sussex—and the old building which houses the admirable butcher—meat, eggs and white turkeys any time of year on a few days' notice—whose hideous clapboard shop front has been giving it an oddly temporary effect for at least two hundred years, there are three shops: the grocer, the draper and the post office. All three sell groceries, green and otherwise, sweets, tobacco, wines and spirits and all have well-stocked deep-freeze compartments. The draper also sells china souvenirs, picture-postcards, clothes, cotton materials and wool. The post office, the largest of them, deals in ironmongery, china, glassware, cosmetics, rubber boots, books and has even, in a rather dim corner at the back behind the bacon, cheese and butter, a small counter with a grid devoted to postal perquisites.

Miss Seeton's cottage, set back from the road and with a small front garden, stands at one end of the village facing down The Street. The name on the gate, Sweetbriars, serves as a postal address for foreigners. People from abroad, anywhere outside a thirty-mile radius, cannot understand that brevity is the essence of good writing. Attacked by verbal voidance they are not content with "Plummergen, Kent" but give the locals such gratuitous information as that they are 'near Brettenden' (6 miles north), or 'near Rye' (5½ miles south) which can delay correspondence up to three days while a blue pencil is found, the 'nearness' removed and the letter re-addressed 'Ashford' (15 miles east), which is 'nearest' from the postal point of view. The cottage's local name at the present time is 'Old Mrs. Bannet's'. Most of the houses and cottages around are known by the name of previous owners; not because of any parochial prejudice against change, but due to practical considerations. Houses are continually bought and sold, occasionally by new-comers to the parish, but more often by the parishioners themselves. As families increase they move into larger accommodation: when the children grow up and the family is scattered, the process is reversed; thus it is not unusual to finish where you started, ending your days in the house where you were born. In Mrs. Bannet's case, that, latterly, her name should have won house-recognition during her lifetime was something of an accolade. It had been deemed presumably that the old lady, when rising eighty and having lived in the same house for some fifty years, was unlikely to shift again until her final move across the road to the cemetery.

The church, part of the existing fabric built before the Norman Conquest, stands modestly from sight at the southern end of The Street, on the opposite side of the road to Old Mrs. Bannet's. Next to it is the vicarage with a garden that adjoins the cemetery. It is a Victorian building of which the unpleasing façade is screened from view by evergreens. Its size, designed for a Victorian family and their retinue, has proved excessive in modern times and it has been divided into two homes with separate entrances. Even so the remaining half is over-large for the present incumbent, the Reverend Arthur Treeves, a bachelor whose maiden sister runs the house for him; she does more, she runs him, all church matters and is, in fact, the power behind the vestment. In speech she is as direct and practical as her brother is wind-tossed and unworldly.

Somewhere along the line Arthur Treeves had lost his faith; not lost in the sense of mislaid, but an erosion, a slow whittling away, a dwindling over the years. He was acutely conscious that he lacked the moral courage to leave the Church and take up other work; but it is not easy, late in life and with no independent means, to change your vocation simply because that calling no longer appeals. He was conscientious and active in the discharge of his duties, but had to steel himself to make his visiting rounds, always in dread that some amongst his parishioners, thinking to please him, might wish to discuss theology; a greensward that had turned to bog beneath his feet, wherein, one day, he feared to be engulfed. The tenets and rules that at twenty had looked such positive solutions to all problems had by now become problems in themselves. He could see so many sides to every question in human behaviour and sympathise with all of them, that the question itself had no answer: every question but one: deliberate unkindness.

"Your coffee, Arthur." Miss Treeves put down the paper and handed him his cup. It was not their own morning paper; there had been such an eager exchange of newspapers throughout the village—"Schoolmistress Scares Stabber" swopped for "Covent Garden Murder Heroine",

23

"Battling Brolly" for "Art Teacher Routs Gang", that no one was now sure whose paper they held. "Don't you think it might be kind to call on this Miss Seeton before tea?"

The Reverend Arthur started, spilling coffee into his saucer. "So soon? Surely not." He sought an excuse for delay; found it. "Next week, perhaps, when she's had time to settle in."

"She's only here for a few weeks, I believe," his sister pointed out. "After all, Mrs. Bannet was an old friend and this is her god-daughter."

"Ah, yes. Yes, of course." He got up, went to the window, looked out: the grass needed cutting. "I must express my sympathy." He returned to the table, stirred his coffee. "When's she coming?"

"She's arrived already. The Bloomers told me she'd be here for lunch."

"For lunch? Here?" He dropped his coffee spoon and looked apprehensively round the room. "Good gracious! I'd no idea …" He made for the door. "I must …"

"Sit down, Arthur, drink your coffee and don't get in such a tiz; we've just finished lunch. Not here for lunch—there for lunch; in her own house," she explained patiently. "Mrs. Bloomer was very kindly going to stay on and have it ready for her. The train was on time; I saw the car arrive."

"She's got a car?" The vicar's mind jumped ahead: The Old People's Party—she could give lifts; The Seaside Outing; endless possibilities. "Can she drive?" he inquired anxiously.

Miss Treeves sighed. "I've no idea. I shouldn't think so. Why don't you listen? Crabbe's car from the garage met her at the station, drove her to the cottage and Bloomer helped her with the luggage."

"Bloomer?" He was cheered; one of his flock in the right place at the right time, doing the right thing. "That's fine. An excellent man with hens. I'll drop by this afternoon and say how sorry we are."

"No, Arthur, no." She spaced her words as though to a child. "Glad. How glad we are to welcome her."

"Yes, that, of course." He finished his coffee and jumped up. "Naturally. Surely you can trust me to say the right thing. But a word about her bereavement is only fitting. After all, we knew her mother well. I buried her."

"Oh, do pay attention, just for once. Her godmother, Arthur. How many more times?"

"Yes, yes, that's what I said," her brother answered testily. "Don't muddle me, Molly." He looked out of the window again: the lawn really did need cutting.

"And try to find out exactly what happened last night."

"Last night?" He turned, surprised. "But she wasn't here, I understood ..."

"Oh, Arthur, it's the talk of the village. It's in all the papers. There was a murder last night in London and Miss Seeton was mixed up in it. The accounts vary, but apparently she hit the man."

For a moment she had his full attention; the vicar was shocked. "It hardly seems a suitable topic," he reproved her.

Molly Treeves was exasperated. "Nonsense. It must have been a most dreadful experience. It would be a kindness to encourage her to talk about it and get it off her mind. If I hadn't got a committee, I'd go myself."

"H'm, yes, I see." He ruminated. "If you put it that way ... Naturally, anything I can do—any way I can help ... I really think you can leave it to me to know what to say."

25

He opened the french windows. "I think some air—I'll get on with mowing the lawn." He escaped. Poor Molly, so well-meaning, but didn't always quite realise … Someone in trouble; there he flattered himself he could be of use. It all sounded most unfortunate. A brawl in London—dubious company—and ending in death, too. Very distressing. Yes, he really did feel he might be of service. To talk it over rationally with someone like himself would give her a different perspective. He trotted off to collect the mowing machine.

His sister watched him with a smile. Poor Arthur, the mere idea of meeting new people did upset him so. Note: she must remember Milk of Magnesia tonight. It was just as well he always took his agitations out on the garden. It kept the place tidy and the exercise was good for him.

"More coffee, anyone?"

"Thank you, m'dear." Without lifting his eyes from the sporting page, Sir George pushed his cup towards Nigel who handed it to his mother. She filled it and gave it back; he gently lifted the bottom of his father's paper and pushed it underneath. Sir George grunted.

Lady Colveden opened wide innocent eyes. "Busy this afternoon?"

Her son's equally wide eyes narrowed. "Why?"

"Just a little errand I thought you might do for me in the village. I meant to go myself only I can't get away, my committee isn't over till five."

"Come off it, Mother darling. When you go all innocent, you're finagling. What are you up to?"

"I'm not up to anything. It's simply that I thought it would be a kindness, that's all. Considering the aunt was our oldest inhabitant and with the niece coming here today, I thought the least we could do was try to make her welcome, take an interest, you know."

The newspaper moved a fraction: Nigel caught his father's eye; it winked. He grinned. "Yes, we know." He finished his coffee, got up and started to stack the luncheon plates. "Do you think I'd be good at welcoming heroines? Anyway, what d'you want me to do? Present her with a gold-plated umbrella, or a Press-cutting book on a salver?"

Lady Colveden considered. "Well, I thought some eggs."

"But she's got hens of her own—at least, she and the Bloomers between them."

"I know, but I can't think of anything else. I ought really to have baked a cake, I suppose, but you know what happens when I do."

There was a strangled noise from behind the newspaper. "We do," her son agreed.

"Well, there you are then." She collected Nigel's cup, took the coffee tray over and pushed it through the kitchen hatch. "I'd have got Mrs. Bloomer to do it, only she changed her day this morning so as to see Miss Seeton in. And you can't go armed with cabbages or cauliflowers, it looks so silly, so what else is there except eggs?"

"A nice bottle of home-made wine?" Nigel joined her at the hatch with the dishes and the plates.

"Don't be revolting."

"Right, eggs it is. What do I do?" he asked. "Crossquestion her, or get a signed statement?"

"Your trouble is you're vulgar." She returned to the table, picked up the cruet and the butter-dish and put them on the bread-board. "It's only natural to sympathise over that

27

dreadful affair last night. How would you feel if you were an elderly spinster, coming to a new place where you knew nobody, after a terrible adventure and you're all alone and nobody calls, nobody cares—I think it's very sad." Sadness was tilting the bread-board; things started to slide.

Nigel reached for it. "Better let me have that before it's overcome."

His mother brightened. "I'll collect the glasses. Of course," she added, "if you manage to find out a little more of what really happened, surely there can't be any harm in that?" Sir George folded his paper and put it down. "Oh, George, you're back with us. How nice. Nigel has just decided to call at Old Mrs. Bannet's this afternoon with some eggs."

"Why?" Sir George took his coffee-cup and went into the kitchen.

His wife carried the glasses to the hatch and poked her head through. "Why? As a gesture of sympathy and welcome, of course." She closed the hatch, retrieved the newspaper and followed the men into the kitchen. She opened the dishwasher. "Will you do the pans in the sink, Nigel, and George, you hand me the rest of the things; I'll stack."

Her husband passed her a pile of plates. "Why eggs?"

"Don't be tiresome, George. Because there isn't anything else, that's why. There was a murder last night." She took the newspaper and started to hunt through it. "You wouldn't know anything about it, you never read the interesting bits, but it's here somewhere; she was in a running fight with the police all round Covent Garden, or something. Old Mrs Bannet's niece, I mean."

He gave her the vegetable dishes. "Second cousin."

"Who's a second cousin, what are you talking about, George?" she accused. "I don't believe you've heard a word I said." She ruffled the paper. "Why do things always disappear when you look for them."

He put the trays on a shelf. "Page one, headline column four."

She made a face at him. "Pig. You'd read it all the time."

"Old Ma B. cousin of mother. Makes Seeton second cousin. Also the old girl's god-daughter."

"Don't be ridiculous, George, how could you possibly know?"

"Asked her."

Nigel hung up the last saucepan. "Father, you've been holding out on us. When did you meet up with the battling brolly?"

"Met her twice. Once visiting Ma B. for the day. Once clearing up after the old girl's death."

"And you've been keeping it from us all this time." She slammed the dishwasher shut. "George, I could kill you."

"Stupid." Sir George bent down, picked up the dispread newspaper, smoothed it, folded it neatly and laid it on the table, "Wife always first suspect. Hire someone. Don't let 'em overcharge."

"No, but honestly, George, knowing her all the time and not a word. What's she like anyway and why didn't you tell us?"

"No murder then."

Nigel snapped his fingers. "I've got it. You know her, you take the eggs."

His father's plump figure headed for the door. "Can't. Going to bed."

"To bed?" Lady Colveden echoed. "What on earth for?"

"Sleep."

"But you can't sleep in the afternoon." All at once she was concerned. "George, you're not ill, are you? No, please tell me what's wrong."

"Rabbits," he told her and shut the door.

"Another cup of tea, Eric?"

"What?" Erica Nuttel looked up from the newspaper. "Yes, thirsty. Dunno why. 'Less there was too much salt in that mock beef. Thought it tasted salty myself." She passed her cup. Mrs. Blaine poured lime tea and handed it back.

Miss Nuttel and Norah Blaine had shared a house for eleven years in the centre of the village opposite the garage; thus ideally situated to watch all the local comings and goings, on foot or otherwise. There was little they didn't know, much they speculated on and a deal they invented about everybody's business. People complained that they spread malicious and unfounded rumours; unfounded was true, but malicious was unfair and for the spreading the people themselves were equally to blame. Faced with any untoward event which had no immediate explanation, an interpretation would present itself which, improved on and garnished in discussion between the two ladies, emerged finally as positive fact. That these intriguing myths lingered long after plain truth had been established was as much the fault of the disciples as it was an error in the preachers of the gospel.

They were dedicated vegetarians, known collectively as The Nuts. Miss Nuttel, tall, angular, with the face of a dark horse, was generally referred to as Nutcrackers. Mrs. Blaine, whose dumpy geniality was belied by the little blackcurrant eyes, was called by everyone Hot Cross Bun; this derived largely from Miss Nuttel's pet name for her of Bunny, but it may have been also a tacit acceptance of the shrewish temper which flared through the placid surface when she was thwarted. Their house, Lilikot, a modern innovation with large plate-glass windows screened by nylon net, was inevitably The Nut House.

"Salty?" Mrs. Blaine did not like criticism. "I can't think why you should say that. You've always liked the mock beef before. It was precisely the same as usual, I followed the recipe exactly. More likely to have been your parsnips, I should say; I thought you were a bit freehanded there. You should know by now parsnips won't stand too much salt, it spoils the sweetness."

"Could be, could be—no need to get into a flap, Bunny. This Seeton woman—" Erica Nuttel jabbed a blunt forefinger at the paper, "think we should call?"

Bunny responded at once. "Oh, yes, do let's, we must find out what really happened. What excuse can we make? I know, we can take her some dandelion wine. We've got plenty and it's full of vitamins."

"Good idea. Stimulating—good as whisky anyday. Better make it last year's—a bad year. Don't suppose she'll know the difference."

"All right, we'll get it out as soon as we've cleared away lunch. When shall we go along to old Mrs. B's? At tea-time? I think this Miss Seeton sounds terribly brave, don't you?"

"Sounds more of a damn fool to me. Not tea-time— too obvious. Wouldn't look well. Better make it three, sharpish."

"Mummy—" Angela raced into the house and flung open the door of the sitting-room. "Mummy, she's here—that woman who's in all the papers this morning."

Mrs. Venning stopped typing. "Have you had anything to eat?"

"No." Angela chucked her coat on to a chair, danced over to the writing-desk, kissed her mother and looked at the pile of paper beside the typewriter. "How's the new book going? Sorry I missed lunch, but I got talking in Brettenden, and one thing and another—oh, you know how it is."

"Nigel Colveden rang you up."

"Nigel? What did he want?"

"He didn't say."

"Oh, well—" She perched on the arm of the sofa, taking cigarettes and matches from her bag. "I'll give him a ring sometime. On the way back I took the car into the village to get her filled and heard all about it from Jack Crabbe, he had to pick her up from the station."

"Hadn't you better get something to eat?"

"Oh, puff food," she threw the match in the fireplace. "I'll get it in a minute." She came back to the desk. "But, Mummy, isn't it ultra about this woman?"

"What woman?"

"Oh, darling," she hugged her mother, "don't be such a fud. I told you—the one who's in the papers, who was mixed up in a murder last night in London, she's here in the village, she arrived just before lunch. I can't wait to meet her, she must know masses of spicy people."

"Who are you talking about?"

"Oh, I don't remember her name, Miss Something-or-other."

Angela collected her coat and tossed it over her shoulder. "But she's taken old mother Bannet's cottage or rather I think it's hers now, or something like that, old Ma B. was a relation of some kind. Let's go and look her up, shall we?"

"Certainly not. We don't know her and from what you say, I should prefer not to. Go and ask Mrs. Fratters to give you some food."

"Oh, all right, but I think you're drab, you never want to do anything spicy." The door banged.

Sonia Venning sighed. She remained still, gazing out of the window. Then, with a shake of her head, she referred to her notes and continued typing.

"Jack the Rabbit jumped nimbly over the stile. He swept off his cap with its tall red feather. He made a courtly bow and held out his paw to little Lucy."

"Well, you're looking better, Miss Angie, I must say." Mrs. Fratters dried her hands on the roller towel and bustled over to switch on the electric kettle. "Thought you were coming down with a cold this morning from the look of you. What d'you want to go and miss your lunch for? Upset your Ma, and not the first time. What's got into you these days? You should have more consideration."

"Oh, don't harp so, Frat." She dropped her coat on the kitchen table, moved over and started to hunt though the store cupboard. "I felt all hung this morning, now I'm fine."

"What you looking for?"

"Some of your apricot jam."

"You don't want jam now, it's not enough." Mrs. Fratters bent down and pulled open the hot-drawer at the bottom of the cooker. "I've been keeping some of the steak 'n' kidney warm for you just in case. There you are now." She dumped the plate on the table and took a knife and fork from the drawer. "You just sit down there and get on with it."

"Yes, yes, in a minute." Angela took a pot of jam from the cupboard, tore a sheet off a memo-pad and sat down at the table. She rummaged in her handbag for a pen and an elastic band. She wrote: "Greetings from Mrs. and Miss Venning. The Meadows, Plummergen." She put the paper round the jampot and slipped the band over it. "There, that's prime."

"Well, I'm off now, dear, so I'll say ta-ta." Mrs. Bloomer came into the living-room, shrugging on her coat. Miss Seeton turned from the french windows which opened on to the lawn. She smiled. "I've washed up and put everything away and laid the tea ready, the cold meat's in the fridge, the rest of the apple-pie's on the table with a cover over it, there's plenty of veg. so you're all right for your supper, unless you fancy something else, if so there's tins—or eggs of course, you can say what you like but it makes a difference when you lay your own, stands to reason, when you buy them there's fresh and fresh, but when you lay your own you know where you are, I've left you six, but if you wanted more for your breakfast, Stan'll be collecting after tea when he waters the hens."

London born and married to a local farmhand, ten years previously, Martha Bloomer had come to clean house twice a week for Mrs. Bannet. Since she lived close by, this was to lead to an arrangement advantageous to them both. As with most houses in the village, the main garden of Mrs. Bannet's cottage lay at the back. The Bloomers lived in one of a row of small dwellings divided from this garden by a narrow lane, a continuation of The Street, which ran down the side of Mrs. Bannet's, over the canal and eventually connected with the main coastal road. The Bloomers suggested that Mrs. Bannet should buy some chickens and provide their feed. Stan Bloomer repaired the disused chicken house, looked after the birds, kept Mrs. Bannet and his own family supplied with eggs and poultry and sold any surplus for his own profit in place of wages. The agreement had proved so satisfactory to both parties that it had spread to flowers, fruit and vegetables.

"Now," Martha concluded, "is there anything else you want, dear, before I go?"

"No, nothing, Martha, thank you. You've done everything possible and I'm more than grateful."

"Right, then off you go to bed, I've put a hot-water bottle in."

"But I can't go to bed in the middle of the day," Miss Seeton protested. "I must unpack and … and …" How curious, now she came to think of it there was nothing really urgent, nothing that couldn't wait.

"And what, dear?" demanded Martha. "You've got out all the things you need for the moment. You get to bed, it's the right place for you, you're looking tired and no wonder."

Miss Seeton was not used to being organised; she found it comforting. "I must confess I am a little tired. I was rather late last night and I'm not used to such a large lunch, delicious as it was." She moved to the door.

Martha followed her into the passage and reached past her to shut the heavy oak door to the cupboard under the stairs. She shot the bolt. "You want to watch it, dear, you nearly walked right into it. The latch doesn't hold right and it swings. You keep it bolted or you'll be getting a nasty knock one of these days. Need to keep your strength up with all your gallivanting about and then the journey on top, so up you go and have a nice lie down, there'll be nobody coming so you won't be disturbed and if they did you wouldn't hear them with your bedroom at the back. Then you can have a nice quiet evening settling in and you'll feel fit as a flea in the morning."

"I think perhaps you're right," Miss Seeton started up the little twisted stairs. "I will lie down, after all. And, Martha—" She stopped and looked down.

"What, dear?"

She still hesitated. "I—I don't know how to thank you. I feel—you and Stan have made me feel—as if I'd come home."

Martha chuckled. "So I should think, what have you done if you haven't? I'll slip out the kitchen way, I need a lettuce for Stan's tea so I'll pull a couple on the way down and pop out by the back gate, it's quicker. Ta-ta, dear, see you Friday if not before."

How lucky she was. Dear Martha, she talked as much as ever: Cousin Flora had maintained that Martha must have been born in the middle of a conversation. In the bed-room she placed her hat and bag on the dressing-table and stood for a moment, discovering the garden. One's own garden. So different from London, not being overlooked. She pulled the curtains to keep the light from her eyes when she lay down, put her coat and skirt on a chair and got into bed. Warm. Comfortable. And so quiet. Nobody to disturb one. So silly to feel guilty, resting in the afternoon. Martha was quite right. It was just what she needed. Sleep.

# Chapter 3

"Well, I must say, Eric, I think it's too peculiar."

"A bit odd, yes."

"It's more than odd, it's peculiar. You don't go to sleep as soon as you've arrived in a place, and in the afternoon, too, unless of course there's a reason. Well, would you?"

"Not myself, no. Not without a reason."

"Do you think she drinks, or something, and is sleeping it off?"

"Could be."

"Oh, Eric, how terrible. We should never have left that dandelion wine, it will only make her worse."

"Might not be. Might be something else. Could be she's ill."

"She can't be too ill, or she'd never have made the journey from London. Though I did just happen to notice the bedroom curtains were drawn, because I slipped down the lane to see. I mean you don't pull your bedroom curtains in the afternoon unless there's some terribly good reason, do you?"

"Not 'less you've something to hide."

"To hide? Yes, that would explain it. But what could she ... ? Oh, Eric, it's too terrible to think of, it couldn't be—it's not possible—drugs, do you think? Could it be that, do you think?"

"Possible, of course. Could be. Could very well be."

The two ladies entered the post office and took their places at the grocery counter.

"It's dreadful to think of, really"—Mrs. Blaine dropped her voice; persons more than six feet away had to strain to listen—"when you remember Mrs. Bannet and imagine how she'd have felt if she'd known."

"Don't forget, Bunny; can't be sure," Miss Nuttel encouraged her.

"Of course not"—her turn to be served had come; she smiled at the assistant. "Two boxes of dates, a packet of digestive biscuits, oh, yes, and a large packet of prunes, please." The shop assistant turned to the shelves; Mrs. Blaine returned to her theme—"but what other explanation is there? I mean, there has to be a reason, Eric, even for the oddest behaviour, doesn't there?"

"Woman's something to hide, certainly," her friend agreed.

"Obviously, and I'm afraid it is the only answer. Of course it would never do to say so. Thank you." She helped the shopgirl to stow her order into her carrier and took out her purse. "There, eight and eightpence halfpenny. Too lucky, I have the exact change. I don't even like thinking about it." She moved away.

Several customers, seed borne on the breath of scandal, had drifted between them and the door. "Oh, good afternoon, Mrs. Goffer, how's your dear little girl, Effie? Not been up to mischief again, I hope. Excuse me—why, it's Mrs. Spice. Looks like keeping fine, doesn't it? But it's too true, I'm afraid," she went on as they threaded their way, "that you're always reading in the papers how the drug habit is increasing everywhere, aren't you, especially in London." The ladies left the shop.

"Wanted more of that puce wool, didn't you?"

"Of course, too silly of me, I nearly forgot." They started across the road. "And anyway it's not puce, it's magenta. I only meant to use it as a border, originally, but I think the all-over pattern is much better, don't you?"

"Don't think it a bit strong against that mustard?"

"Oh no, Eric, mustard's all the thing at the moment, but it needs a strong contrast to go with it. I can't think what Mrs. Venning was doing sending a pot of jam."

"Jam?"

"Yes, you remember those pots of jam, they were all from people in the village and I just happened to notice the card on the apricot one said: 'Greetings from Mrs. and Miss Venning'."

"A bit odd for the Venning."

"It's too peculiar. After all, Mrs. Venning never goes any-where these days, you practically never see her. I wish we could find out why. I mean it's too funny when you think she used to be quite gay and go out a lot and then she suddenly stopped. I feel sorry for poor little Angela."

"Not so little as all that. Seventeen or eighteen, must be."

"Yes, I suppose she must be about that by now. She's so gay always."

"Too gay, I'd say. Or too moody. Too much up and down altogether. Hysterical type, if you ask me."

"Oh, nonsense, Eric, she's just young and high spirited and that always leads to moments of depression. I was just like her as a girl. You wouldn't understand because you've always been the blunt, forthright type. I used to think she and Nigel Colveden would eventually make a match."

"Doubt it. She's always gadding about in that little car. Drives too fast. And that club outside Brettenden she's always at, that's too fast, too."

"Well, it must be terribly dull for her now that they never invite people to the house any more. That's what makes it so funny that Mrs. Venning should send greetings to a newcomer." They stopped to look in the draper's window. "Do you see, they've got that mango chutney we've always had to get in Brettenden. Do you think perhaps they've met in London?"

"Could be. The Venning used to go to London a lot. To see her publishers, or so she said." A bell pinged as she pushed the door.

"Those silly children's books of hers—" Norah Blaine followed Miss Nuttel into the shop. "Good afternoon, Mrs. Welsted," she greeted the proprietress.

"Good afternoon, Mrs. Blaine."

"—yes, that would explain it, if they knew each other in London." She reached the counter. "I need some more of that magenta wool."

"Yes, Mrs. Blaine, how much?"

"Of course, with what we now know about Miss S., it's too obvious in that dreadful affair last night, there must have been more in it than meets the eye. How much?" she echoed. "Well, you see, I've decided to do the patterned, instead of the plain with the border. I mean, Eric, you don't get mixed up in murders and things without good reason, do you?"

Mrs. Welsted called her daughter. "Margery, how many ounces of magenta will Mrs. Blaine need if she's doing the patterned twin-set?"

"Matter of fact, Bunny, I don't get mixed up with murders at all myself." Miss Nuttel held out a pair of stout gardening gloves. "How much?"

"Ten and six," said Mrs. Welsted, "and very good value."

"I'll take 'em."

Margery Welsted finished her calculations. "Mrs. Blaine will need sixteen ounces."

"Well, there you are, Eric," Mrs. Blaine exclaimed, "it must have been some of those terrible people she'd be bound to know, to do with—you know what—and that sort of thing always leads to trouble."

"There's the wool and gloves." Mrs. Welsted handed her the parcel. "I'll credit any of the mustard wool that's over to your account. Is there anything else you want, Mrs. Blaine?"

"No, nothing else, thank you, Mrs. Welsted." She accepted the parcel and turned to go. "In my opinion that would explain about Mrs. V., I mean why she suddenly took to staying at home and seeing no one. If you want to know what I think," she held the door open, "I think Mrs. V.'s frightened."

Miss Seeton put on her hat. Yes, that coxcomb effect in stiff ribbon gave it character, she considered. Half-past three; goodness, she'd slept over an hour and a half. How right Martha had been; she felt much less tired now. Some air, yes, that's what she needed and with the sun shining, it was an ideal moment: she must go round the garden. She went down the stairs.

She'd always liked the cottage; but it was curious how much more personal—no, to be honest—how much more lovable a place became when it belonged to you, when you got that first little awareness that, perhaps, you belonged to it. Good gracious, what were all those? She turned from the kitchen door and moved down the passage. Beside the telephone, on the narrow table just inside the front door, were several parcels with notes stuck into the wrapping. These weren't here before. Who in the world … had people been calling while she was asleep? Oh dear, she hoped they hadn't thought her rude not to have answered the door. She began to read the labels. But she didn't know any of these people. It was plain, and naturally one understood, it was for cousin Flora's sake; she must have been much loved in the village. But, for all that, to make her, a stranger, welcome like this was so kind—so kind … There was a knock at the door. She opened it.

"Miss—er—Seeton, is it?"

"Yes?"

"I'm—er—Treeves, your—the vicar."

"How do you do, but how nice of you to call." She stood back. "Won't you come in?"

"Oh—er—I—" Arthur Treeves hesitated, then took the plunge. "How very good of you. I—er, that is, it's so nice to meet you."

Miss Seeton closed the door and started for the kitchen. "Can I offer you some tea?"

"Tea? Oh no, I wouldn't dream of putting you to the trouble."

"But it's no trouble."

"Oh well, in that case—but, no, my sister wouldn't approve."

"Your sister?" She stopped in surprise. "Doesn't approve of tea?"

"Oh no, good heavens, no. No, she drinks a lot, she lives with me. She wouldn't approve of my imposing on you."

"But it's not an imposition, I promise you. It's all laid ready. I'll just put the kettle on, if you'd like to go into the sitting-room."

She repaired to the kitchen, switched on the electric kettle and came back to find the vicar still hovering in the sitting-room doorway. He stood aside, bumping into the hall table.

"Ah, been shopping, I see," he remarked as he followed her in. "What do you think of our local stores?"

"No, I haven't been out. I've only just seen those parcels and I'm rather overcome; they're presents, I think, a form of greeting from some of the people in the village, I imagine. I was about to read the cards when you called." She sat in an arm-chair near the fireplace. "Won't you sit down?"

"Ah," he brightened as he perched on the edge of the chair opposite her, "that shows generosity of spirit, that pleases me very much. That's how I see people, you know—like to see them, that is—warm-hearted, well-intentioned friends. Friends," he assured her, "that's what people should be. And to see a true example of it here, makes me very happy indeed." The brightness clouded. "But, dear me, I'm forgetting one of the chief reasons for my call. To offer our condolences, my sister's and mine, and our sympathy in your loss. Your grandmother was an old and valued friend."

Miss Seeton smiled. "Not grand—, Mr. Treeves, but god—."

Not Grand, but God? The vicar flinched. A Deist possibly? And fanatical at that. "Quite, quite." He jumped to his feet. "We all have our own views, beliefs, faith—call it what you will. Live and let live is my creed. Dogma and doctrine may differ, but at bottom—or perhaps I should say, heart—I like to feel we're all the same. And now I really must go, I mustn't keep you."

"But, vicar, your tea? The kettle must be on the boil." She rose.

"Tea? Oh no, certainly not. Wouldn't dream of giving you the trouble." He hurried from the room. "I'm late already, I must fly. Good-bye, Miss—er——" He grabbed the latch. "So nice to have met." He threw open the door. "Oh …" Confronted by a policeman in uniform, he stepped back hastily, knocking against the table; the parcels teetered, Miss Seeton was in time to save them. "I'm so sorry, clumsy of me."

"It's all right, there's no damage done. Excuse me for one minute, I must switch off the kettle." She hastened to the kitchen.

"Ah, Potter," the vicar was geniality itself—law and order had come to his rescue, "you were looking for me?"

"No, sir."

"No?" Pure chance then—providence was abetting his flight. "In that case I must be off. Nothing I can do, eh? I quite thought for a moment you were coming here."

"I was, sir. A Miss Seeton is here, I understand."

"Seeton?" The Rev. Arthur hesitated—and was lost. "Yes, that's right. But you don't want her, my boy, there's nothing she can do for you, she's only just arrived." But a small doubt was burgeoning in his mind. Something Molly had said. Something he should have said. Something—what was it—London? Trouble of some sort. Something distressing. And one of his people. He must stay. He might be needed; perhaps be able to help.

Miss Seeton came back. "I'm so sorry to have kept you waiting, I had to open the kitchen door to clear the steam."

"Miss Seeton?" P.C. Potter inquired.

"Yes?"

"I've been instructed to give you notice of the date of the proceedings that you are required to attend."

"Proceedings, Potter?" The vicar took up mental cudgels and waved them. "I can't have this ..."

"It's all right, Mr. Treeves," Miss Seeton reassured him, "I think I understand."

"But I don't." He was stern. "Attend what? Explain yourself, Potter."

"The inquest, sir. Miss Seeton is required as witness."

Arthur Treeves was shaken. "Inquest? Good heavens, but nobody's died." But somebody had. Wasn't that what Molly had said? Somebody dead in a brawl in London. And this Miss Seeton—oh dear, oh dear. Doubtless not wholly to blame. Extenuating circumstances, if only one understood. His duty was plain. He must go with her; lend support. "When and where is this inquest, Potter?"

"The day after tomorrow, sir, at eleven-thirty. I took down the details for you here." He handed a paper to Miss Seeton.

"Eleven-thirty, good heavens, that means an early train. Leave it to me, Potter, we shall be there."

"No, not you, Mr. Treeves," Miss Seeton protested, "I wouldn't hear of it. They told me it would be quite short. It's all most unfortunate."

"The more reason for me to be there."

"No, really, it's very kind of you, but ..."

"Not another word; I go with you. I'll let you know tomorrow the time of the train and I'll order a car from

45

Crabbe's. Well, I must go on my way. In the meantime, don't let yourself dwell on this unhappy affair. We must face things as they come." He went on his way and P.C. Potter went with him. "All most unfortunate," murmured the vicar, "but I feel it is my duty to be there."

"I'm sure she'll be glad of your company, sir. Between you and me, the London chaps, the Yard in fact, has instructed me to keep an eye on her." The pride of direct contact with the head of all headquarters shone in every button.

"Have they?" His unhappiest surmises appeared established facts. He shook his head gloomily. "Have they indeed." The vicar walked home deep in thought.

"Miss Seeton?"

Nigel, having failed to get any response to his knock, came round the side of the cottage and into the main garden. Like so many of the afternoon's callers, he could have left his parents' offering with a note, but he had his own reasons for wanting to see Miss Seeton personally and his mother's commission had given him the excuse he needed. At first he had thought the garden to be empty and that both Miss Seeton and his luck were out, but noticing a movement behind the shrubs which backed the herbaceous border at the end of the lawn and screened the hen-houses and vegetable garden from view, he crossed the grass to investigate. He found that it was Miss Seeton's hat and not the wing of a bird as he had at first thought.

"My name's Colveden," he continued as she turned to face him. "I hope you don't mind me butting in. There was no answer at the door, so I wandered round the side and saw you were down here. You know my father, I believe."

"Yes, indeed, I met Sir George twice, I think. How do you do, Mr. Colveden."

"Nigel. Actually I'm my mother's stand-in at the moment. She would have floated in herself, to see you touch down, but she was committed this afternoon and as father's up to his pillow in rabbits there's only me, I'm afraid—with a dozen eggs."

"Oh, no, Mr. Colveden, it's very kind and please thank Lady Colveden most sincerely, but I can't accept any more, it's so embarrassing and especially eggs, you see," she indicated the hen-house, "we lay our own."

For one split but glorious second Nigel was vouchsafed a vision: Miss Seeton, in that hat, enthroned on an outsized nesting-box, led her hens in a count-down—three ... two ... one ... The vision faded. Nigel guffawed. "Sorry," he gulped, "a passing thought. But, apropos the hens, that wall at the back of the hen-house should be at least three feet higher, you know."

Miss Seeton studied it. Now one came to examine it, that back wall was quite a bit lower than the side wall down the lane. Of course, with that tree in the corner, one didn't really notice it at first; in fact she doubted if she ever would have noticed it if it hadn't been pointed out. It was only just higher than the roofs of the hen-houses themselves and not as high as those wire cages in front of them. She looked back at the house: ah yes, that would be the reason; so as not to break the view sloping down to the trees bordering the canal and over the fields beyond. Then, surely, it was better left as it was. Why make it higher? "Why?" she asked.

Nigel laughed. "Some of the local talent hop over egg-hunting. Crazes up the hens; you'd think it was foxes at least and makes Stan Bloomer madder than a hornet."

47

"Oh, I see. That's why Martha keeps the second key to that side door and insists we keep it locked."

"I say ..." He stopped. It was ridiculous. She was so completely different from anything he'd expected. From what he'd read in the papers he'd imagined ... now he came to think of it he didn't really know what he had imagined. Probably some rather overbearing, militant female; positive, an organiser, a boss-type, in fact. Certainly nothing like this little old innocent. And he'd been so sure somehow. The Miss Seeton of his imagination had looked like a possible answer to his problem at last. But this Miss Seeton wouldn't even understand the problem or, if she did, would be likely to have a fit. To his embarrassment he realised she was looking at him expectantly, waiting for him to go on. He was pained and surprised, while still trying to think of some social pleasantry to cover the awkward pause, when he heard his own voice asking, "Do you mind if I ask you something?"

"I shouldn't think so, Mr. Colveden."

"These detectives—you know, the Yard men you met in London ..."

"I beg your pardon?" She was startled.

"Well——" Nigel was a little jolted. "Well, I mean, you did, didn't you?"

She gazed at him in astonishment. "But I don't see ... how could you possibly know about that?"

"Everybody knows about it, it's in all the papers." The penny dropped. "Good Lord, didn't you know?"

"Certainly not. No, I ... oh dear, how dreadful—the newspapers." For the first time she saw last night's events objectively in relation to herself. "How vulgar. Then that's why, this morning ... how stupid of me not to realise. I never thought"—her repugnance grew—"those photographers, too—how very shocking." For her the worst had happened. "It's so vulgar," she repeated helplessly.

"I say, I'm awfully sorry to've upset you. I'd no idea you didn't realise ..."

"It's all right, Mr. Colveden. It's my own stupidity, I'm afraid. You see I'm not used to that sort of thing. It never occurred to me ... oh dear."

Nigel almost laughed. It was incredible. She hadn't even realised her own predicament. And he'd been thinking of asking her help in his. But there was a chance he might be able to achieve his object without involving her at all. "They'll be coming down here to see you?" he asked casually. "The detectives, I mean."

"Good gracious, no. Why on earth should they?"

"No, of course not. I'd just imagined there'd be interviews, statements and all that sort of thing. But naturally you'd have done all that already. Silly of me."

He tossed the subject lightly away. It landed on Miss Seeton's ear with the sad thud of despair. She studied his profile. "What's the matter, Mr. Colveden? And why did you wish to meet these detectives?"

"I?" said Nigel innocently. "Oh, no reason. I was vaguely interested, that's all. I don't particularly want to meet them."

She continued to watch him. "No, naturally not."

That did it. The same words—the same tone of voice. He was back in the headmistress's study at his kindergarten accused of catapulting ink pellets round the classroom. His denials had been met by her slightly bored "No, naturally not". The contemptuous indifference of the adult agreeing with a tiresome child. Now, as then, he promptly blurted out the truth.

"I'm in a mess," he stated. "Or rather I'm not, but a friend of mine is. Or soon will be. And I'm a bit boxed in down here, there's no one I can ask advice from, no one I can even discuss it with."

"But surely, Sir George …"

"Lord no, my father's the last person, as you'll see in a minute."

Miss Seeton collected herself and made for the cottage. "Have you had tea, Mr. Colveden?"

"Tea?" Nigel stood bewildered, then loped after her. "Tea? No, why?"

"Because," she said practically, "I haven't and I don't know about you, but I could do with it. We can go and make tea, then we can take it outside and sit in the sun and you can tell me anything you want to in comfort."

She entered the kitchen, and switched on the kettle which, after its recent and abortive boiling, began encouraging noises almost at once. "I'm afraid, from what you say, I can't imagine I shall be of any use." She selected the larger of the two gift cakes and began to unwrap it. "I don't think I know anything about messes, as you call them, or what to do when you're in them." She put the cake on a plate, added it to the tea-tray and surveyed the result: bread and butter, biscuits, jam, sandwiches, small cakes, large cake—that should be ample. Martha's idea of tea for one was her idea of supper for two. But the young needed a lot of food. "It does help sometimes to talk over one's troubles. It's saying them aloud that helps, I think. And sometimes they shrink. But then, of course, sometimes they don't," she added with honesty. "As for anything to do with the police," she continued, "I'd be no use at all. I've never had anything to do with them." Looking up she saw Nigel's left eyebrow rise as he hovered in the doorway; she turned slightly pink and laughed. "Well, hardly ever." The kettle was boiling, she picked up the teapot. "You take those folding chairs and table out while I make the tea."

Sitting in the sun, with the food spread before him and told to help himself, Nigel found he was hungry. Miss Seeton put down her cup and refilled it.

"Now, Mr. Colveden ..."

"Nigel, please."

"Very well, Nigel, what is this trouble or mess and why can't you discuss it with your father or anyone you know?"

"I suppose," he answered slowly, "—I suppose it's just because I do know them. The whole thing's so local—that's the trouble. Father would be the ideal person to talk to, of course, but I can't as things stand because he's a J.P. and I'd be putting him in an impossible position later as a magistrate if I told him all I know now. I mean, if I do manage to keep this friend of mine out of it when it busts wide open, as it's bound to, father can't very well sit in judgement on a case knowing that someone else should have been involved and that I'm covering up for them."

Miss Seeton nodded. "I see. This friend of yours has done something actually against the law?"

"And how," Nigel agreed. He took up the cake knife and toyed with it, brooding on the result of his one attempt to lecture Sonia Venning on the duties of motherhood and the upbringing of daughters. Talk about a packet of deep-frozen raspberries. "To mind his own business"—nicely chilled;

"Since when did he presume——"—served on ice; "Did he really imagine"—in fact frost on everything. Miss Seeton, wise in her experience with children, said nothing further. She waited. Nigel, in face of her cool gaze—no judgement there, merely detached sympathy and interest—fell. "It's a girl I know," he stated abruptly. "She's very young, only seventeen and irresponsible." He grinned at her, stuck the knife into the cake and cut it. "All right, I know; so I'm only a year older, but I'm not irresponsible. I've known her for years; she was only six when she and her mother came here to live, so we've sort of grown up together and I can't let her go on as she is without doing something about it. Anyway, it's all her mother's fault. Mrs. Venning ..."

"Venning?" Miss Seeton sat up. "Wait, I'm almost sure— yes, a Mrs. and Miss Venning left a pot of jam this afternoon."

"You mean——" Nigel put down his cake and gazed at her. "You mean you know them then?"

"No, indeed," she disclaimed, "but several people left things and I'm afraid I missed them because I was asleep. But there were messages and one of them was from a Mrs. and Miss Venning."

"From Mrs. Venning?" He frowned. "That's strange, she never goes out these days, never sees people, or anything, if she can help it. That's the whole cause of the trouble; that's why Angie's gone wild. To sort of compensate, I suppose."

"But, surely, Nigel, there can't be many opportunities for wildness in a small village."

"Little you know." He laughed shortly. "Well, you wouldn't know about our local troubles, but there's been a lot of vandalism lately round the Brettenden district. And it's getting serious. There've been two robberies I know of and in the second, last week, a man and his wife were badly beaten up."

"But this is quite, quite dreadful." She was scandalised; and in the country too—it made it even worse. "But surely if you say you know—I mean the police …"

"I know, all right, but I doubt I could prove it. And even if I could, I'm hamstrung. You see Angie was with them in the car both times."

"But you must go to the police," she insisted, "surely you see that. I mean it's quite dreadful, robbery and violence. You say this man and his wife were hurt. You can't leave it like that. Even without proof you must tell them what you know. Quite apart from the danger to other people, it makes you partly responsible for anything else that may happen."

He stared down towards the canal, unseeing. "Think I don't know that? But would you go to the police if your sister was involved—that's pretty well what Angie is to me—without making one final effort to get her out of it before the balloon goes up?"

"A final effort?" She seized on this. "You've done something already? You've tried speaking to her, reasoning with her?"

He smiled ruefully. "Yes, I've tried both those. I've also tried shouting and yelling at her. I think I've tried everything but a whip where Angie is concerned. We quarrel every time we meet and now she avoids me like the plague. A few months ago the police raided The Singing Swan—that's the club where they all meet: hot music and supposedly soft drinks—the other side of Brettenden, beyond Les Marys, but they got nowhere, the police I mean. They raided again last week—the night before the robbery with the beating up, a night when Angie wasn't there—because they'd had an anonymous tip-off. But no dice—everything as innocent as all pie." He shrugged. "Maybe the club got an anonymous tip-off too; I wouldn't know."

"But how did you find out about the information the police had, did one of them tell you? I would have imagined they would have kept very quiet about that sort of thing."

"I would have hoped so, too." There was a wry twist to his mouth. "I found out about it quite easily by phoning the tip myself, did a break-and-enter at the Vennings' garage, put the car out of action and then managed to hijack Angie by offering her a lift to The Singing Swan and driving flat out for Brighton." He gave a reminiscent chuckle. "We had an unholy row." He stood up, restless, stuffed his hands in his pockets and began to pace. "I'd known there was something on for that night from a slip she'd tried to cover up and from the way she was behaving, all glitter-eyed and galvanised."

"Oh dear," she watched him, helpless, "I don't know what to say. You seem to have done everything possible and more. I don't see what else you can do—on your own, that is."

"Nor do I. It's no good trying to do anything more locally, as they appear to get wind of it somehow. And I guess my next move's likely to end in me being beaten up by Angie's little playmates. I thought," he turned to her, "if it was possible to interest Scotland Yard in any way and set up something from a distance, it might work. But if there's no chance of their coming down here," he sat down, leaning forward, eager, "I suppose you couldn't have a word with the fellow in charge of your case, could you?—say you'd seen someone like this Lebel type round the S.S."

"Oh no," she exclaimed in dismay, "I couldn't possibly do that, it wouldn't be true."

"It could be," he argued, "or near enough. From the description I read this morning he sounds very much in their line at the S.S. I borrow Mother's car and hang around there quite a lot, trying to keep an eye on things. You could come with me one night and from a distance you could mistake any of the boys for this Lebel."

Miss Seeton shook her head and got up. "No, Nigel, I'm sorry, I'm afraid it's impossible. It would be untrue and misleading the police. I think it would be very wrong. Also I don't know about these things, but can Scotland Yard interfere without being asked to?" She saw his defeated expression. It seemed such a shame, so unfair that he should get involved in something like this. She did wish Sir George … But no. She agreed with Nigel, that was quite impossible. As a magistrate he could never countenance any suppression of charges against Miss Venning if, as Nigel seemed to fear, such charges could legally be made. But to appeal to her, of all people … What could she do? She hated the idea of being so useless. It was ridiculous, of course, but she felt as if she'd betrayed a trust. "The only thing I can think of," she began tentatively, "and what I will do if you like—if you think it might help at all—is to tell Superintendent Delphick what you've told me without, of course, mentioning your name or Miss Venning in any way, and explain the difficulties as far as I can and ask his advice. He told me he would be at the inquest so I shall see him then. He's such a nice man, so understanding, that I'm sure if he can make a suggestion, or if there is any way in which he can help, I'm quite certain that he will."

# Chapter 4

There was little conversation on the return journey after the inquest. The morning event, though short as Superintendent Delphick had foreseen and the verdict of murder against César Lebel a foregone conclusion, had given both Miss Seeton and the vicar food for thought.

Miss Seeton had been grateful to Nigel Colveden for making clear to her the notoriety she had brought upon herself. She had wisely decided to endure what she could not avoid and to ignore it so far as possible. She had resolved to be careful and to do nothing which could give rise to further comment, happily unaware that her own nature was bound to betray her. Little as she realised it, Miss Seeton was situation-prone. She was conventional to the core, but natural and logical behaviour in unconventional situations can appear the height of eccentricity to onlookers.

When the coroner had praised her bravery and gallantry, she had winced at the mention of her name in public but otherwise had shut her ears to what he said. After the verdict the superintendent had asked her to lunch. Finding her accompanied by the vicar, he had included him in the invitation. The vicar, however, excused himself, saying that he would meet her at the station in time for the train.

It had been a delightful lunch with a charming companion who, with a mixture of tact and frankness, had largely succeeded in reconciling her to the part she had played. He did make her see that publicity is a penalty you sometimes have to pay for doing what you believe to be right, but he failed to make her realise that she herself might still be in danger and that, in spite of the coroner's verdict, the case against Lebel was liable to collapse if she was no longer available as a witness. The vicar's absence had made it easy for her to broach the subject of The Singing Swan. The superintendent had surprised her by his interest. Instead of polite and rather offhand attention which was what she had expected, he had cross-questioned her closely, embarrassingly closely, and she had been hard put to it to give the facts as Nigel had told them, without mentioning names, or Angela Venning's connection with the club. However, she felt she had accomplished this and had been much gratified by his promise that he would quietly look into the matter and see that something was done.

Superintendent Delphick, too, was pleased. He found Miss Seeton's company refreshing and had managed to keep her away from the Press. Obviously there would be talk in her own village, but it didn't seem likely that such talk would reach London.

There was, indeed, talk in her own village. The superintendent was not to know that the talkers were rapidly splitting into two main parties: those who favoured Miss Seeton as the agent of a London dope ring come down to have it out—though what 'it' was, was so far unspecified—with Mrs. Venning: and those that looked upon her as a victim of the drug habit who, having failed in her battle for further supplies in London, had arrived to see the chief supplier, Sonia Venning, in person and insist upon her rights.

Delphick had detailed a man to travel down on the same train as Miss Seeton and to keep a sharp outlook for any sign that she was being followed, so he felt that he had done all that was humanly possible to ensure that her address was not known to any interested party. He had reckoned without the vicar.

For Arthur Treeves the inquest had been a humiliating revelation. He had come to stand by one of his parishioners in trouble who, probably through thoughtlessness or lack of experience, had got into bad company and might need a guiding hand, would need moral support, only to find that he was escorting the heroine of the hour. He felt deeply stressed at the thought of his previous unworthy misgivings and could not but feel that his sister was partly to blame for misleading him. Between embarrassment and humility he was quite unable to face the lunch that the superintendent had proposed; he needed time to sort out his thoughts and formulate a fitting apology to her for his baseless suspicions. Consequently, when the Press who had noticed him sitting with Miss Seeton in the court, being baulked of their quarry by the superintendent, had descended on him in a flock like pigeons on a crumb, he had been only too glad to seize on this opportunity for atonement and say how proud they were in Plummergen of Miss Seeton's arrival in their midst; that her example was an inspiration to them all, shining even more brightly than that of her grandmother who had lived amongst them so long and whose cottage she now inhabited. Thereby at one stroke undoing all the superintendent's planning of the last few days.

They were nearing Brettenden before Arthur Treeves finally resolved his problem and had the exact formula of his apology worded in his mind. He cleared his throat.

"I—er—h'rm," said the vicar. Miss Seeton looked inquiry. "I—er—feel … that is to say I must own—or rather it is my duty to tell you that it's all most unfortunate," he explained.

"Oh, I do so agree," she replied, "most unfortunate, but I do feel myself to blame. I see now that if one interferes in people's affairs, one must be prepared to take the consequences. It's horrid of course but it's over. I don't want to talk about it any more. I've quite made up my mind. I simply shan't read the newspapers for the next few days and then everyone will have forgotten about it and I shall be able to, too."

She found Nigel at the cottage when she got back. For a moment her heart sank. She was tired and would have liked to have been alone. But after her first qualms she found his gay take-over comforting. He had the kettle on the boil and refused to let her talk until he had taken her hat and coat, ensconced her in an armchair, made and brought in the tea which was laid ready in the sitting-room, poured it and seen her drink her first cup. He had even brought some plain chocolate biscuits, by chance a favourite of hers, as his own contribution. She leaned back in her chair and smiled at him: he was so very eager, but thoughtful, too. It wasn't fair to keep him in suspense. She must collect her thoughts and try to remember everything Superintendent Delphick had said; even though, when you summed it up, it didn't really amount to a great deal.

Nigel forestalled her. "Hope you don't mind me pinching tea off you two days running and making myself at home, but I thought you might be tired when you got back so I went down to see Martha and persuaded her to let me in and get things ready."

"I'm most grateful," murmured Miss Seeton.

He chortled. "You should be. Martha had made up her mind to be here herself when you got back, but she's in one of her Grand Slams and the whole thing was so noisy I'm afraid I told her you were expecting me and got her to go away."

"Oh, dear." She sighed. "What's the matter with Martha? And what is a Grand Slam?"

"Haven't you met her in one of her Slams?" She shook her head. "Good Lord, you haven't lived. 'If people tittle-tattle about people, what people need'—that would be the people of the first part," he explained—"'and what people are likely to get is a piece of somebody's mind.' The somebody of the third part being Martha, of course. All to the accompaniment of a lot of slamming doors, pans, brushes, anything to hand. If only she'd go and slam the people she's got it in for instead of everything within hearing, it would be a lot quieter and much less wearing. It might even do some good."

She laughed. "It's silly of me, but I hadn't realised you knew Martha so well."

"Oh, help, yes. Martha's been doing for us at The Hall for years. I've known her since I was knee-high to nothing."

"What is it that's so upset Martha?"

"Gossip," said Nigel darkly, and then looked sheepish. "About you, I'm afraid. Based on some splendid misreading of the newspapers. I know," he hurried on, seeing her expression, "don't let it get you down, it'll blow over. Meanwhile the village gossips are having themselves a fancy-dress ball and, as far as I can make out from Martha, have linked you with Mrs. Venning in sundry dark deeds in the woodshed."

"But I haven't even met Mrs. Venning," she insisted.

"Trifles like that don't make any difference. At a guess," he continued, "that would be the Nuts—Miss Nuttel and Mrs. Blaine to you. They're the parish substitute for a Hollywood scandal sheet. There's nothing unpleasant they can't brew up at the Nut House—and throw in a few adders' tongues for good measure. They must have 'just happened to notice' the pot of jam here that afternoon when they left their own tiny token, and 'just happened to peek' at the message with it. I wouldn't be surprised if they didn't 'just happen to taste' the jam as well."

Miss Seeton sat forward, put down her cup and pushed the tea-trolley to one side. "Well, it can't be helped. What you want to hear is what the superintendent said."

Nigel grinned. "Yes, I do a bit," he admitted, "but I was trying not to rush you."

They discussed exhaustively all that Miss Seeton had said to Superintendent Delphick, all that he had said to her and all the possible meanings, double-meanings, and innuendos that could have lain behind or between everything that either of them had said. Something had been done: a move made; a little nebulous, perhaps, but at least something, and Nigel felt cheered. He pushed the trolley through to the kitchen, his offer to help wash up was firmly refused, so he took himself off, assuring her that if his mother's M.G. sports was available, he would continue his watch on the club in the hopes of being able to gather more information.

After clearing up, Miss Seeton decided that she would have a light supper and go to bed early because she was tired. But first she must do her routine. She repaired to her bedroom. She put a folded travelling-rug in a corner against the wall, removed her shoes and her dress, got out her book and sat down. Opening the volume of *Yoga and Younger Every Day* she was faced with a photograph of a gentleman doing a solo imitation of the statue of the Trojan priest, Laocöon, and his children fighting with the serpents. "The Star Posture— advanced Yoga." A little too advanced perhaps. In any case, even if she could ever achieve it, she saw no advantage in being able to put one leg behind the back of her head, with the foot on the opposite shoulder. Such a strain. She turned the pages back. Ah yes, here she was—"The Headstand". "Put a clock in a place where you can see it. Close your eyes and breathe slowly." Really, what were they thinking of? What place did they imagine you could see a clock when you were upside-down with your eyes closed. Miss Seeton set her egg-timer to ring in three minutes. She knelt down, clasped her hands, placed her head against them on the floor, arched her body, walked her feet forward, then launched herself at the wall.

Superintendent Delphick pushed the overflowing out-tray to one side and regarded the empty in-tray with satisfaction. There was a knock on the door. In answer to "Yes", a constable entered carrying a batch of papers, he dumped these in the in-tray, collected those in the out-tray, saluted and left the office. Heroically Delphick refrained from comment.

"Bob."

Sergeant Ranger put down the file he was studying. "Sir?"

"Get me Ashford on the line, will you? A personal call to Chief Inspector Brinton. If he's not in, scrub it."

He glanced quickly through the new lot of papers, decided there was nothing that couldn't wait, took a notebook from the drawer of his desk and began to write. After a few moments the sergeant interrupted him.

"Chief Inspector Brinton on the line, sir."

Delphick picked up his receiver. "Chris ... Yes, too long, that's your fault. Either things are too quiet your end or you're too efficient... . Don't say you've grown modest since I last saw you... . Tell me, Chris, strictly between ourselves, have you any gen on The Singing Swan down your way? ... Come, come, you forget, my spies are everywhere... ." For some time the superintendent listened in silence, taking occasional notes. "I see," he said at last, "interesting. But you've no idea where the leak was—supposing there was one? ... No, no, not yet, but I have a feeling it may. Anyway, if it does, I'll let you know, and thanks a lot ... See you." He hung up and looked across at the sergeant. "Bob, you don't by any chance know anybody living at Brettenden, I suppose—or even better, at Les Marys?"

"I've never heard of either of 'em, sir."

"Pity. A spot of leave, to visit friends or an ageing relative would have done you good. But I've an idea that gap in your geographical knowledge may be filled shortly."

"Where are they, sir?"

"In Kent, Bob, in Kent. The one adjoins the other and both are near to Plummergen."

"Plummergen? But that's where Miss Seeton ... Don't tell me she's biffed anybody else, sir."

"Don't be common, Bob. The Miss Seetons of this world don't biff people; they indicate displeasure with the ferrule of an umbrella." He paused and added thoughtfully: "But when they lie, that interests me."

"I can imagine Miss Seeton doing almost anything, sir, but not lying."

"You're quite right, it would be against her principles. Prevaricate is the proper word. We lunched together after the inquest and she told me a lot of flapdoodle, serious, but flapdoodle all the same, about a club called The Singing Swan near Brettenden. She knows nothing about it—only what she's been told. But for some reason she's not telling me all she's been told. But the reason why she was told—and then told me—and the reason why she's not telling me all she was told, are what interests me if you follow me."

"No, sir."

"She's covering up for someone who's covering up for someone. And that, in case you didn't know it, is intelligent deduction."

Bob Ranger considered The Oracle and Miss Seeton having lunch together. His imagination boggled. If The Oracle was going to get matey with Miss Seeton he wondered if he himself should apply for a transfer.

"You look worried, Bob," his superior commented.

"Well, sir, you can be bad enough on your own—you say things. But she not only says 'em, she does 'em."

"You sorrow me, Bob. You should cultivate Miss Seeton."

"God forbid, sir."

"I mean it. It's another gap in your education. Until you can learn to understand her, you'll get nowhere as a detective. She's everybody's conscience, Bob—the universal maiden aunt, cousin or sister. Humanity's backbone. Throughout history she's gone to the stake for you again and again; not with any sense of heroism, but as a matter of principle and because it would never occur to her to do anything else. She scrubs for you, sews for you, cooks for you, nurses you and is your unfailing support in times of trouble."

The sergeant pictured himself supported by Miss Seeton in times of trouble: a transfer wasn't enough—emigration—Canada, perhaps. The Mounties. After all they always got their man. It said nothing about women.

Delphick threw down his pen and sat back. "The whole dam' case is so nebulous. I know those two girls' killings are connected—same method; both prostitutes, both drug addicts, both pushers. We've Lebel pinned for the second, if only we could find him, but nothing to connect him or Prévost with the first girl. What's the good of feelings if you can't find sufficient evidence to support them. Just have to wait for the next move," he finished in exasperation.

A telephone rang.

"Chief Superintendent Gosslin, sir."

Delphick reached for the telephone. "Delphick here, sir… . The evening papers? No, not yet, sir… ." He listened with a gathering frown as the instrument quacked. Finally: "No, nothing. Just one of those things… . Thanks a lot, sir." He put the receiver back. "Blast!"

"What's happened, sir?"

"Nothing yet," Delphick said savagely. "But all my puerile precautions to keep Miss Seeton's whereabouts under wraps have been blown sky high by that doddering half-wit, the vicar of Plummergen. He came up with Miss Seeton as escort, refused to join us afterwards and then, it appears, improved his shining lunch-hour by giving an interview to the Press. I gather he gave her family's life history, her address and what time she would be at home to visiting assassins—in fact everything except details of the parking facilities. The Chief's just seen the late editions and it's all in the reports on the inquest. So the next move may come any time. In Kent, I guess."

Nigel lurked. He was chilly and uncomfortable and he felt like a badly cast minor conspirator in an indifferent melo-drama, but he continued to lurk, grateful that he had had the forethought to bring a couple of garden cushions. For such information as he could gather he had been wont to rely on occasional visits to the club, the overhearing of unconsid-ered scraps of conversation and above all on his translation of Angela Venning's moods and ill-considered chatter. Now he was aware that his appearance at the club was viewed with suspicion by those few whom he, in turn, suspected; a suspicion which might turn ugly at any time. Since the Brighton episode Angela had avoided him. Lurking was the only solution.

There were five boys and two girls whom he had pin-pointed as the main trouble-makers. Two of the boys owned or had the use of cars. During the last week he had contented himself with parking some way off and then followed at a distance one of these or Angela's, whichever seemed the most promising. He had decided that if another break-in was tried, either he would light up the scene with his own head-lights in the hope of frightening them off, attempt to join in himself or go for the police, according to what seemed best at the time. What he would do if Angela was again directly involved he had never quite faced. This watching and wait-ing had produced nothing except the conviction that the monotonous and tiring role of a private investigator was not for him. Individuals had been dropped at their homes, good nights screamed and the cars parked for the night. The group appeared to be resting on its laurels.

That drugs in some sort were in question he knew; but whether it was merely a matter of pep pills or whether it embraced anything more serious he had been unable to discover. In particular how far this had been carried in Angela's case was his chief worry. Some months before, she had persuaded him to try a couple of what she called her boosters. He had taken the pills and had awaited the effect with interest, thinking the experience might make him understand her better and so be more effective in dealing with her. It had not helped. Either the dose was too strong or he was allergic. He had just begun to feel slightly dizzy and relaxed, when he realised that the relaxation was of a different order and he was sick.

The car park to the club was fenced by wooden palings. Behind the fence Nigel squatted under close-growing shrubs. The leaves were damp with dew; the ground likewise; he had the definite impression that creatures from above, spiders, earwigs and their ilk, were on their way down via his collar, while creepers from below, ants, centipedes and their kind, were on their way up by way of his trouser legs, for a social convention around his midriff. He was, as stated, chilly; he was also wet and he tickled.

Disappointed, after Miss Seeton's report, that armies of policemen were not already on the march, a little reflection had shown him that the fact that the Yard had questioned her closely and had assured her that something would be done, was a big step forward. This encouragement had determined him to keep vigil as long as he could, or as long as his mother's complacency about lending him her M.G. lasted. Her only comment that afternoon had been that with a husband who slept by day and shot rabbits by night and a son who fly-by-nighted in her car, she was not only grass-widow and grass-mother but was left stranded on the grass as well.

Over the fence Angela's car was parked next to one of the suspect's with the other not far away, so he felt he was in a good position to hear anything of interest. The club was emptying, it was getting late. The door was thrown open and in the shaft of light a shrill group of youngsters clattered down the steps. The door closed and the dark figures, growing clearer as moonlight took over from electricity, headed volubly towards Nigel's hiding-place.

"Who you think you kidd'n, chick?" The accent was outer Odeon. "Heroines for gossakes, down here? You kidd'n?"

The voice of one he didn't know. Nigel peered through his leafy screen. Yes, there were two he hadn't seen before. What he'd told Miss Seeton had been quite right. Any of these seven youths could be mistaken for Lebel, judging from his picture in the papers, even at fairly close range.

"But it's true, I tell you." Angela's voice, light and clear and feverish.

"No more'n six mile away," one of the other girls chimed in. "C'mon."

"A real live heroine—now I guess that's the kinda broad I'd like t'see. What say we go call on her—look her up like?"

"That's a spicy idea, I've wanted to meet her," cried Angela above the squeals of delight from the other two girls.

Four of the boys swelled the chorus, but one held back. "Don't be so daft. It's late enough," he pointed out, "she'll be sleeping."

"Well, for gossakes we c'n wake her up. She's not deaf or sump'n?"

There were shouts of approval. "Yes, why not?" agreed Angela. "Let's get going."

"Tell you you're daft," the other boy countered. "Her place's right on The Street. We'll have the whole village out on us."

This started an argument that the new-comer quelled. "I guess I'd still like to see where a slap-up heroine lives," he persisted. "If they go t'bed so goddam early can't we jest drive by? We c'n always dip our lights in salute or sump'n."

"Come on then," called Angela. "I'll lead. We'll go round the marsh and come up from the back. That'll leave you heading your right way and you can carry on." She ran for her car, jumped in and started the engine. The others bundled noisily into the remaining vehicles except for the new-comer who, accompanied by his silent companion, headed for a car parked near the entrance.

Nigel held his breath as Angela's car shot out into the roadway swinging right with protesting tyres, followed by the two locals, the stranger's car bringing up the rear. He scrambled from his hiding-place, made a quick survey—no one in sight—threw the cushions over the fence, vaulted it, scooped them up and ran for the M.G. Should he phone the police? Once that gang worked themselves up there was no knowing what they might do or where they'd stop. On the other hand they didn't seem too bad tonight and the one he knew as Art had been putting a brake on the proceedings—at least he didn't want the whole village roused. It should be all right, he decided, and, as they were going the long way round, if he got weaving he ought to be there nearly as soon as they. If everything was quiet he could carry on home without stopping. Yes. He'd risk it. He reached the car, flung the cushions in the back and leapt into the driving-seat.

Good gracious, what was that?

Miss Seeton, suddenly awake, found it difficult to orient herself. Of course. It was the hens. What a noise! Oh dear. Really. She got quickly out of bed, into her slippers, pulled her dressing-gown round her and hurried down the stairs. Without stopping to put on a light she instinctively snatched her umbrella from the drip-tray in the passage as she passed, unlocked the kitchen door and sped down the garden. No, really. It was too tiresome of them. Of course Nigel had warned her. Upsetting the hens like this. Well, she'd soon put a stop to it. Thank heavens, there was enough moonlight to see one's way. Poor Stan; he'd be so cross.

The squawking from the hen-houses continued unabated. Miss Seeton arrived at the runs. She beat on the wire door with her umbrella.

"Stop that," she called. "Stop that at once, do you hear me?"

"Sure, lady. I hear you."

She gasped. A shadow moved forward, reached through the wire and unhooked the door. With the moon behind him Miss Seeton could see little but a dark shape muffled in a coat, a hat pulled low. But the moon shone on the barrel of the pistol he held.

"Now, just take it nice and easy, lady. Back to the house and no noise, see."

"Don't be so childish," she snapped. "And put that toy away at once or I shall send for the police." She brought her umbrella down smartly on his wrist.

There was a flash. A sharp blast. There was a howl of mingled rage and pain. The gun fell.

"Oh dear," cried Miss Seeton in startled dismay. "I'm so sorry, I'd no idea … I hope you didn't hurt yourself." She was talking to the air. The figure, dancing in wild abandon on one foot while clutching the other, had hurled itself at the hen-house, heaved itself on to the roof and vanished over the wall.

There was a thud, a yelp, a curse. There were stumbling footsteps, running footsteps. Windows thrown up, doors thrown open. The hens redoubled their efforts in the face of competition.

People calling: "What is it?" "Murder." "Shots." A man's voice: "Quick, for gossakes, quick." Two loud reports, yells of pain. Doors slamming, engine revving. And trumpet-tongued above the tumult, Sir George's triumphant bellow:

"Got him, by God—a barrel a buttock."

Two speeding cars, one close behind the other, headlights at full coming round the second curve of the S-bend ahead. This would be the Brettenden contingent, Nigel decided. That was a relief. Nothing could have happened. To have got this far in the time meant that the cars hadn't even stopped. Angie must have turned off already down the lane to The Meadows and the other car would be on its way back to wherever it had come from.

He slowed down and took a powerful torch and dark glasses from the dashboard. He had been prepared for their ditching game for some time, but this was likely to be his first chance to test his counter-measures. As the cars came into the straight he put on the glasses and dipped his lights. They didn't. He smiled: so they were going to try their usual trick. He'd seen them at it often enough, but he'd generally been behind them.

The leading car, headlights blinding, drove straight at him. At the last moment when he knew they'd veer, Nigel eased his off-wheels from the narrow road on to the grass verge, flipped up his headlights and shone his torch full on his opponent's windscreen. There was a yell of dismay and curses, followed by the heartening sound of tearing branches and rending metal. One in the ditch and one to play.

Nigel, his lights and torch still on, drove straight by the second car which had slowed to give its mate room to manœuvre, resisted the temptation to take a swipe at the head sticking out of the driver's window and screeching abuse, flung his glasses and torch on the seat beside him, switched off his lights and drove for the bend, thanking the moon above for light enough to steer his course.

Once round the first curve he flicked his lights on again and exulted. Hoist with their own petard. For once some devils had been given a slice of their due. They'd no chance to read his number-plate nor was there room to turn and follow. In any event they'd be too busy getting their fellow-travellers out of the ditch.

A few moments later he drove happily into Plummergen. All quiet at Miss Seeton's; no lights—good. He was turning right at the end of The Street into Marsh Road, heading for home when the hen-house war broke out behind him. He slammed on his brakes, reversed into a gateway and raced back.

Windows were lighting in many houses. He cut his engine in front of Miss Seeton's and leapt out. What a racket! The hens—of course, it must be down there. He ran forward. As he reached it, the entrance to the lane beside Miss Seeton's flooded with light. A car rocketed out and down The Street. The stranger's car. He rushed back to his own, jumped in, slewed the M.G. round to follow, jammed on his brakes again to avoid by inches the stocky figure of his father as Sir George ran from the lane, double-barrelled shotgun at the ready. Nigel threw open the passenger door, catching a glimpse of the vicar cantering out into the road, arms and nightshirt flapping, a ghost from the graveyard, shouting: "Stop, thieves, stop!"

Sir George stepped into the car without breaking stride and slammed the door. Nigel raced through his gear changes. Light poured from open doorways, torches flashed, people in strange array ran out, ran back, waved hands, waved pokers, brooms and sticks, all shouted and the mechanised cavalry swept into action as the M.G. roared down the centre of The Street in pursuit of its quarry, with Sir George, gun still at the ready above the windscreen, standing braced for battle.

# Chapter 5

The men at Rytham Hall slept late the next morning.

"Anybody up yet?"

"Up, but not down, m'lady."

"Boiled eggs," said Lady Colveden.

She closed the front door. Thank heavens, it was one of Martha's days; someone to help with the lunch. She took her shopping through to the kitchen and began to lay a tray. Ten past ten. One egg and two pieces of toast each; that was quite enough as late as this. She heard the hoover start. Right, if Martha was doing the dining-room, they could have it in the morning-room. For the hundredth time she wished they could eat in the kitchen, but with all the plumbing arranged under the only window it wasn't feasible. To alter it apparently meant a major operation.

They both looked a bit sheepish, she decided, as they finished their eggs and toast—like schoolboys caught out in a peccadillo. So they should, from the stories going round the village—and the state of her M.G. Beyond the over-casual good mornings, followed by eye-avoidance, nothing so far had been said. She handed them tea.

"Did you have a good night?" she asked brightly.

Sir George spluttered. Nigel choked. Both hurriedly put down their cups. They looked at each other, then at her. Sir George gave a strangled hiccup, Nigel whooped and they collapsed in helpless merriment.

It was most unfair. For a few seconds, Lady Colveden managed to maintain her air of innocent inquiry, but an irrepressible giggle tricked her and she joined the happy throng. There was a knock and Martha put her head round the door.

"The police've come for you," she announced.

That finished them. Superintendent Delphick entering followed by his sergeant had a fleeting impression that they should have been carrying pails of fish to throw to the sea-lions.

Order partially restored, introductions made, Martha Bloomer dispatched for coffee and biscuits and the detectives seated, apologies were offered.

"No, please," disclaimed Delphick, "the police so seldom get an uproarious reception; it's a refreshing change. It was primarily Miss Seeton we came to see," he added.

"Wrong house," croaked Sir George.

"No," murmured his wife weakly, "right house, wrong time. She'll be back for lunch." She collected herself. "Please, Superintendent, you must forgive us. I know it's very serious, but I think we're all a little overwrought this morning. My husband and son have only just come down to breakfast so we've had no chance yet to catch up on each other's activities. I've heard various versions of theirs in the village—all colourful and dramatic and all, I'm sure, inaccurate—but they don't even know that Miss Seeton came back here for the rest of the night."

"You fetched her, m'dear?"

"Yes, George, in that monstrous estate wagon of yours, as my own car was out on another mission at the time."

"I'm sorry about the M.G., Mother, I'm afraid we …"

"It's all right," she assured her son with a smile. "I quite understand. At least …" the edge of her smile was a little keener, "I'm sure I shall—some time. I went into Crabbe's garage this morning, when I saw the car wasn't back, to ask if they knew anything about it. They'd found it outside when they opened up, with your note under the wiper, and got busy on it straight away. They'd already beaten the dents out of the wing, mended the lights and were putting the bumper back on. Crabbe told me there's nothing serious and he hopes to bring it back before lunch."

"Yes," commented Delphick, "we heard something of that particular episode from the Ashford police. I'll go into that later if I may. The only firm fact I've gathered so far is that there was a disturbance last night and as this disturbance would appear to have centred round Miss Seeton"—Bob Ranger let out an audible sigh—"we were called in since there was the obvious possibility that there might be a connection with the case in which she is already involved as a witness. The Ashford police told us that it was very late when they brought Sir George and Mr. Colveden back here, so we didn't like to bother you too early. We called at Miss Seeton's but she was out, so we had a look round her place to get the lie of the land. Then we were informed by a Miss Treeves—that would be the vicar's sister, I take it—that Miss Seeton was staying here. Miss Treeves, an eye-witness I understand, very kindly gave us her account of last night's affair. And the vicar, another eyewitness, very kindly gave us his. Several people came forward, all eye-witnesses, and they very kindly gave us theirs. The accounts differ: ranging from the stealing of eggs, through Miss Seeton threatening to shoot up the village, to a full-scale invasion by troops. So we came here, I'm afraid a little earlier than we intended, to try and get some facts to fit these fancies. If you'll bear with me, we would be very grateful for a full statement from each of you in turn which should put us in the picture. I think it would probably be simplest, if that's all right with you, Lady Colveden, if we heard your side of it first as you seem to have been more on the fringe of the affair."

Fringe? That irked her. "Well, I didn't really do anything, Superintendent," she replied airily. "I just went over there and disarmed her and brought her home with me."

Sergeant Ranger was startled into speech. "Disarmed her? You mean you took her umbrella away?"

"Certainly not," Lady Colveden answered; "she had that in her other hand. I took her pistol away."

"Good God!" said Sir George.

Having made her point, Lady Colveden gave them a straightforward account of the little she knew at first hand of the night's events.

Rytham Hall, up a winding drive off Marsh Road, was about five hundred yards from Miss Seeton's cottage. Lady Colveden had been reading in bed. Soon after midnight she remembered being vaguely conscious of fowls making a noises somewhere and then a crack that might have been a shot. She had gone to the window and leaned out. She had heard distant cries and then two more reports, followed by screams and somebody shouting. It had sounded, but she couldn't be sure, like her husband's voice. She had dressed quickly and, seeing that her own car was not yet back, had taken Sir George's. Arriving at The Street, she had found several people converging on Miss Seeton's cottage, some with torches although there was enough moonlight to see by. The vicar had rushed up, trying to persuade her to give him a lift in pursuit of the thieves who had driven off only a few moments before. She had seen no point in careering round the countryside with the Reverend Arthur in his nightshirt and no slippers—she did hope Molly Treeves had made him take a hot bath when he got back—after an unknown car travelling in an equally unknown direction.

Miss Seeton's hens were still vociferously indicating the centre of the disturbance so she had gone round the cottage and down the garden to find Mr. and Mrs. Bloomer, Martha armed with a broom and Stan with a bill-hook in one hand and a torch in the other, standing as bodyguards to Miss Seeton who, in her dressing-gown and leaning on her umbrella, was holding a pistol aimed at a cluster of bewildered villagers gathered by the side door in the wall, with the beam of Stan's torch illuminating them as if for target practice. She had broken up this tableau, told everybody to go home, taken Miss Seeton's pistol away from her and persuaded her to return to the cottage, pack a few things for the night and come back with her to the Hall. She had made up the spare bed and put in two hot-waterbottles, Miss Seeton and she both had veganin and hot milk and both had gone to bed and to sleep.

"Not, I'm afraid," Lady Colveden concluded with a look at her husband and her son, "in the tradition of high heroism and romantic endeavour, but I like to think it was practical."

"Practical and very wise," agreed Delphick. Lady Colveden glowed. So much for that 'fringe'. "There is just one point which is not quite clear," he continued. "What did you do with the pistol?"

"The pistol?" She was disconcerted. "I—er … George," she rounded on her husband, "if you laugh I swear I'll leave you. And Nigel, if you snigger, I'll make you pay for the M.G.'s repairs." She gazed back at the superintendent, wide-eyed. "How awful. I'm not quite sure," she confessed.

"Well, don't worry about it," Delphick reassured her. "There was no reason for it to seem important to you—at the time. But I think we ought to find it. It can't be far away. Let's see. You didn't put it down to help Miss Seeton pack?"

Lady Colveden reflected. "No, I don't think so. At least I don't remember doing so."

"No? Then you certainly wouldn't want it when you were driving. You might have put it in the back of the car."

"Superintendent, you're brilliant," she exclaimed. "I remember now: that's exactly what I did do. I put Miss Seeton's case in the back and threw the pistol in after it."

Sir George went hot; Nigel cold. Delphick gave an inward shudder. It had, presumably, been fired. Therefore on the same presumption the safety-catch was off. What with Miss Seeton waving it at the villagers and Lady Colveden tossing it lightly among the luggage, it was a miracle that no one had been killed.

"Is the garage locked?" he asked. She shook her head. "Sergeant." Bob Ranger left the room.

"Well, if no one wants me any more I'll go and help Martha prepare lunch," suggested Lady Colveden.

"No, nothing further at the moment, Lady Colveden, except to thank you for a very clear statement and also to thank you for your prompt action in removing Miss Seeton from the danger zone last night. I'd be grateful if you'd tell her that we'll call and see her after lunch, if we may."

"Certainly, Superintendent. And see if you can't persuade her to stop here. She's talking about going back to her cottage this afternoon. Apropos, Nigel, if she does insist on going back—and always presuming that my car has been returned by then—will it be all right for me to use it? Or had you any further manœuvres in mind?"

"It's all right, m'dear. The boy can drive. Decided it's time he had a car of his own."

"What a good idea, George. I suggest an armoured car—or a tank." Her exit was spoilt by her bumping into the sergeant as he entered with the coffee-tray. "Oh, good," she remarked, seeing the automatic pistol lying on a clean handkerchief beside a plate of biscuits. "You've found Miss Seeton's gun all right. Thank goodness for that. I suppose," she added wistfully, "it would be against the regulations for you to slip me a copy of your notes later on. It appears to be my only chance of ever finding out what everybody got up to last night."

The door closed. The sergeant put his burden on the table, picked up the handkerchief and took the pistol to his superior.

"I've put the safety on, sir. There won't be any fingerprints of course, or if there are they'll be everybody else's but."

Sir George sat up. "Safety-catch?"

The cups of coffee Nigel was bringing them wobbled in their saucers. "Do you mean they've been running round with that thing and chucking it about cocked?"

"I'm afraid so, Mr. Colveden, but as fortunately nothing's happened, it might be better not to mention it. No point in spreading unnecessary alarm and despondency. Now, Sir George. Where were you exactly when the shooting started?"

"Down by the canal."

"With a gun?"

"Rabbitin'."

"Ah yes, that would be just beyond Miss Seeton's boundary. Do you get many rabbits down there, sir?" Sir George reddened. Delphick smiled. "Would I be right in assuming that you have been patrolling—I beg your pardon—rabbiting just these last nights since Miss Seeton's arrival?"

Nigel leaned forward. "Good Lord, Father, why didn't you tell me? We could have shared watches."

Sir George avoided his son's eye. "Thought you had other things to do." Nigel subsided.

The superintendent watched them with interest. How alike they were in some ways. But if they must form themselves into a kind of private Home Guard, why not have a discussion and plan their campaign together? Sir George evidently knew what his son had been doing; whatever that might be. No, wait. Did he know? Perhaps suspected was a better word. Nothing had been said openly. Yes. That must be the clue. Nothing said. But why? Major-General Sir George Colveden, Bart, K.C.B., D.S.O., J.P. Yes, J.P., that could be it. Sir George was a local magistrate. In which case, though he might be able to ignore suspicion, he could not overlook actual knowledge. Which meant … All that rigmarole of Miss Seeton's about the club. Yes, Nigel was probably her informant. And all that idiotic covering up must mean that some friend of his was involved and his father mustn't know. How complicated. Also stupid and tiresome. But it did shed an obscure light on certain aspects and meant, if he was to get anything out of the boy, he'd have to question him on his own. He repressed a sigh. Well, back to his muttons. He addressed Sir George.

"We had, of course, asked the local police to keep an eye open."

" 'Course. Good lad, Potter. But only one of him. Can't be everywhere."

"Precisely. Which is why I should like to express my most sincere thanks for your sudden interest in rabbits. You said you were down by the canal."

"Four cars came over the bridge. Went up the lane. Last one stopped. Dam' chickens started quacking. Moved in closer. Heard a pistol-shot. 'Fore I could get there, chap fell over the wall. Began to run, had a limp."

"A limp? H'm, he could have twisted his ankle jumping down. Can you describe him?"

"Never saw him. Back view, overcoat and hat. Let him have both barrels. Peppered his bottom—tell from the way he jumped. Youngish from his movements. Reached the car and was off before I could reload. Chased up the lane after him. People comin' out everywhere, they'd see to Miss Seeton. Thought it important to catch the car, shoot its tyres off. Found my son there: entrained and got crackin' after 'em."

\* \* \*

After them. Which way now? Maidstone road through Brettenden, or the Ashford by Ham Street. Hoped the boy knew. Apparently did. Without hesitating, Nigel took the right-hand fork for Ashford. Sir George narrowed his eyes to slits against the rush of air. Wished he'd got goggles. Huh? Oh, good boy. He took the pair of dark glasses Nigel handed to him and put them on. No use sitting down, if they got a view he'd never have time to scramble up again. Silly little car this of Meg's; stand up or lie down, no proper sitting. He braced himself against the back of the seat and hoped they'd hit no bumps.

This couldn't go on. Have to put a stop to it. So far as Nigel was concerned anyway. All very well for Meg to say not to interfere, let the boy try his own methods and as it was her car he was using she ought to have most say. He smiled briefly, remembering his wife's logic. But it wouldn't do—too serious. Let Angie go to hell her own way. That had been her car, the first of those four tonight. Knew the sound of it. Admit it hadn't stopped, but she'd been there all right, he'd bet on that. Silly little chit, needed discipline. Why the devil didn't Sonia … ? Something very wrong there, nice woman once. Angie, too, nice little girl. But lately … These youngsters, doing everything for kicks. But caring not a damn about the people they kicked.

"Car ahead," shouted Nigel.

Sir George peered forward. Yes, headlights. Travelling fast. He bent down. "Know the number?" he yelled.

"No. I think I'd know the car."

Think. Not good enough. Silly ass. Couldn't go shooting up cars on spec.

"Try to overtake. Get level. Force 'em into the side and stop 'em. Can't keep apologisin' for shootin' up wrong cars."

He straightened. Light coming from the side at the crossroads ahead. Damn these hedges. Growing brighter. Instinctively his son eased his foot.

"Keep goin'," howled Sir George. "Ours major road; they've got halt sign, have to stop. Keep goin'. You"—he bawled into the night—"you, you goddamned …" A car shot from the side road, turning on two wheels into the straight in front of them. "Halt. Halt, you fools. Our road, Major roa—"

His voice was drowned by the wail of a siren and the skidding scream of the M.G.'s tyres as Nigel, between braking down and changing down, fought for control. Sir George dropped his gun which exploded forlornly into the hedge, and clung to seat and windscreen as with a twanging crunch they slithered inexorably into the illuminated sign at the back of the other car. There was a tinkle of glass and POLICE vanished as the light went out. There was a reek of petrol.

Both drivers sprang into the road. Recriminations were stayed by the sound of an engine. A lonely figure on a Velocette puttered into view. Waved on by the police driver, P.C. Potter, the only mobile pursuer left, helmet straight and wireless antenna riding high, passed with a salute and phut-phutted on his way.

"A first-class man, Potter," commented the superintendent. "He was taking particulars of an accident about a mile from the village, on what I believe is the Brettenden road, when he heard distant shots. Having been warned to expect trouble he radioed a report, alerting patrol cars north and south of Plummergen. On the outskirts of the village he was told that two cars had been seen streaking north. As they hadn't passed him, it had to be the Ashford road, so he followed up as best he could."

"No luck?" asked Sir George.

"I'm afraid not. The car you hit sent messages and road blocks were tried, but there was never much hope. There were too many possible routes and too little description available. Incidentally, Sir George, the driver of the car you unfortunately immobilised admits that he was late in sounding his siren, forgetting that the hedgerow would have hidden the flashing of his roof-light. He gives your son full marks for avoiding a serious accident."

"Generous," said Sir George.

Delphick smiled. "Give credit where it's due. The car wasn't too badly damaged, I take it?"

"No," agreed Nigel. "It looked a bit sorry for itself. I'm afraid the police car came off worst with a bashed petrol tank. We told them everything we could and then they radioed for a tow for us, because a wing was binding and one headlight was a goner. We dropped the car off outside Crabbe's garage in the village and the tow brought us on home before going back for the police car."

Delphick got up. "Well, thank you, Sir George. I think that's all quite clear and I needn't keep you any longer. We only need Mr. Colveden's statement, then that's all till we can get in touch with Miss Seeton. Just one thing," he added as Sir George opened the door, "grateful as we are for your help, I'm bound in duty to remind you that the licence for your shotgun is for sporting purposes and not, in this country, for big game however pepperworthy. Whatever one's personal opinion on the types we are hunting, the law insists they are treated as being on the police reserve and not as vermin." He grinned. "However, I feel there is little likelihood of a complaint being lodged in this case."

Sir George gave a short bark of laughter and left the room. The superintendent did not return to his chair. He moved to the window and stayed there for a time admiring the garden.

Beautifully planned and, considering the difficulties these days, amazingly well kept. Whoever had planted the trees bordering that long vista must have done so with loving care and forethought. Brown, copper, scarlet oak, the crimson and purple of maples, dark gold and primrose yellow hazing to the blues of cedar and eucalyptus, interspersed with every shade of green. And below, the present owners had extended and sharpened this massed colouring in the flower-beds, shrubs and borders that framed the sweep of lawn.

Bob Ranger watched him warily. Not a good sign with The Oracle, this long pause.

Delphick swung back to the room. "Now, Mr. Colveden,"— yes, he was right, the sergeant concluded, he knew that tone; the storm signals were out—"your name I know, your address is here, your occupation is what?"

Nigel stared. "Occupation?" This curt tone was a surprise after the superintendent's urbane and friendly manner of a few moments ago. "Occupation?" he repeated, "I'm still training."

"For what?"

"Agriculture. I go back in a fortnight. Father's done wonders with putting the farm on its feet, but it doesn't make money and it could be made to. Pay its way properly, I mean. And that's what I intend to do."

"Hard work."

"So's anything else, but this happens to be work I like."

"You're the only child then?"

"No, I have an older sister. She's married and lives in London."

"During this training period then you're not at home a great deal. Is that right?"

"Not this last year, no. Only for holidays."

"Your arrival on the scene last night was timely."

"I—I suppose it was."

"It was. Why?"

"Why? I was on my way home."

"From where?"

"Brettenden."

"Where in Brettenden?"

"I'd been out."

"Obviously. Where?"

"At a place outside Les Marys."

"Its name?"

"Does that matter?" Nigel was becoming resentful under the terse questioning.

"If it didn't I shouldn't ask. You were I should imagine in a club called The Singing Swan."

"I wasn't in it."

"Don't let's indulge in sophistry," rapped Delphick. "Where exactly where you?"

"Under some bushes behind the car park."

"Alone?"

"Of course I was alone. What do you suppose?"

"I suppose nothing, Mr. Colveden. I'm trying to get facts. You were alone under some bushes behind a car park. Why? Or is it part of your agricultural training?"

"I was trying to keep a watch, if you must know."

"On whom?"

87

"I don't know all their names," he snapped in exasperation. "They're a group that use the club a lot. One of them's called Art and another Micky or Nicky, I'm not sure which. And one of the girls's called Sue."

"Allow me to help you." Delphick went to the table where his sergeant was sitting and picked up a piece of paper. "Susan Frith, Diana Dean, Arthur Grant, Michael Hughes, Percy Davis, James Trugg, John Hart. Were they all there?"

Nigel gaped. "If those are their names, yes. They all came out together."

"Anybody else?"

"No," he answered quickly, thinking of Angela—then: "that is, yes, there were two other fellows whom I didn't know. They were talking to them, but they weren't with them. I mean they had a car of their own. I got the idea they didn't belong down here."

"What gave you this idea?"

"Only that one of them spoke in a terrible sort of Cockney version of American. Also I think something was said about their car—that it would be heading back in the right direction—which gave me the impression they came from a distance."

"Can you describe them?"

"Not really, no. The moon wasn't all that bright and I didn't notice. One of the girls was wearing a dress, but otherwise they all looked much the same. Tight trousers, loose jackets and mops of hair."

"Were either of the two you didn't know wearing a hat and overcoat?"

"No … Oh, wait, one of them, I think, was carrying a coat."

"Did you hear much of what was said?"

"Yes, they were quite near me, I could hear all right. There was some talk about Miss Seeton. It sounded as if they'd been reading about it in the papers and the Cockney American said he'd like to meet a heroine. But the one called Art said they couldn't, it was too late. So in the end they decided to drive round the other side of the marsh and come back up the lane past Miss Seeton's cottage. Oh, yes, that's when somebody said that they'd be on their right road."

"Who said that?"

Nigel frowned as if trying to remember. This needed care. "I don't know. That is I'm not sure. One of the girls, I think."

"What happened then?"

"They drove off."

"All four cars?"

"Yes ... no," he floundered, then recovered, "three cars. The Brettenden lot have only got two cars. The other fellows had a car over near the entrance. I didn't see it clearly. It was a dark saloon, that's all I know."

"Oh, no, Mr. Colveden, not all you know," said Delphick enigmatically. "Aware, then, that these slightly—irresponsible shall we say?—friends of yours," he glanced at the list of names he was still holding ...

"They're not friends of mine," retorted Nigel.

"... these slightly irresponsible acquaintances were converging on the cottage of an elderly woman living alone, it didn't occur to you to give her a friendly warning; nor, even more to the point, get in touch with the police. You just," he dropped the list back on the table, "went home."

"No ..." Nigel began to protest.

Delphick over-rode him. "No. You took time off, on the way home, to play dangerous road games with these acquaintances of yours and put one of their cars in a ditch."

For a moment, Nigel was too startled to speak. How could he know about that? How could he have found it out so quickly anyway? He thought back over what had been said. There was nothing … one minute—an accident on the Brettenden Road with Potter taking particulars. That must be it. They'd guessed it was his car. But they couldn't know for certain. "You couldn't possibly prove that," he stated.

"If it interested me at all, or was of the slightest consequence, I should imagine it could be proved a dozen ways. The prints of your tyres on the verge should be enough."

"All right, then," Nigel answered savagely, "I did ditch them. I only wish I'd been able to ditch the other car as well. And it's not a game, as you seem to think. They tried to put me off the road, but they didn't expect me to be ready for them. I've watched them do it to other people before."

"I see. So you not only lie about under hedges listening to other people's conversations, you watch them too—you follow them about."

He didn't think he liked this, decided Bob Ranger. Not a bit. What was The Oracle getting at? After all, this youngster had tried. Done pretty well, too, he would have thought. They were always asking the public to have a go. Well, he'd had one. And look where it was getting him. The Oracle was forgetting that the boy was only a boy. Reaching back to that callow horizon of eighteen from the staid maturity of twenty-eight, Bob readily admitted that if he'd copped The Oracle in this mood at that age, he'd have rolled himself up in the carpet by now and had himself carried away.

"Perhaps you'd like to explain why you've been watching and following these people."

It was pathetic, Nigel thought, that he'd actually wanted to meet these Scotland Yard detectives. Wanted to see them. Wanted to talk to them. Wanted to ask their help. Wanted … With regard to this particular specimen at all events, he must have been out of his miniature mind. He'd even been eager to give them information. After a session with this type, he wouldn't give them the time of day.

"Well, Mr. Colveden?"

Why had he been following them? No harm in telling them that, he supposed. "Because they're—well, I can't prove it, therefore it's not a fact, so I don't see how it can help you. But I know—sorry, wrong again, it's just another of my ideas—that they've started raiding people's houses. Stealing."

"Sarcasm and rudeness aren't exactly helpful."

"I quite agree," retorted Nigel, "but I don't see why it should be one-way traffic."

"Whatever you may suspect these people of doing, from the little you've told me so far you appear to have no grounds for these suspicions."

"No grounds?" he exclaimed. "Well, if you don't want to believe anything else, what about last night?"

"Last night, you yourself, Mr. Colveden, helped to give them an unshakeable alibi. Both cars were a mile away on the Brettenden Road, one of them in a ditch. The occupants of those cars were making statements to a police constable at the time when the shooting took place. They could not possibly be concerned. It sounds to me far more likely that you're trying to get your own back on these young-sters for some imagined slight or injury; including, unless

I'm mistaken, trying to involve the police in your private vendetta by anonymous telephone warnings of events that never took place."

"Never took place?" Nigel's fury was beginning to loosen his tongue. "What about that poor wretched man and his wife who were robbed and beaten up the next night. I suppose that was fancy too."

"A specific accusation." Delphick returned to his chair, sat down, stretched his legs out and stuffed his hands in his pockets. "At last. Now, perhaps, we shall get somewhere. How do you know these same people were involved? Were you there?"

"No, I wasn't." He was sullen. "Didn't even know what had happened till next day."

Delphick frowned. "I saw the file on that case this morning. No mention of your evidence. If you knew so much, why didn't you go openly to the police?"

"A fat lot of good that would have done."

"Yes, it would. The only reasonable conclusion, if you're not involved yourself, is that you're trying to protect someone who is."

"I ..."

"Don't bother to protest. I've neither the time nor the inclination to play ring-around-Rosie with you. If I'm right you won't admit it and in any case I shall very soon find out. One thing I wish to make quite clear: I do not like," deliberately he spaced out the four words: "vicious, shallow little hooligans who endanger other people's lives and property simply for their own entertainment. They mostly take drugs to foster their excitement and become as filthy in their persons as they are in their habits. I know it's correct these days to look upon them as sick and in need of help and treatment, but if you'd seen as much of them as I have and of the effects of their mischief, you'd realise that with the number of worthwhile people in the world, it's a waste of time and money to try and save the scum. Better and simpler to flush it down the drain where it belongs."

Nigel sprang up stammering with rage. "How d-dare you speak like that. You kn-know nothing about it. Just b-because you're older you think you can s-solve all the world's problems, know the answer to everybody's t-troubles. What about the p-parents? Have a look at them for a change. You—you couldn't even imagine what it's like to be young, with no brother or father or sister, with nobody except a mother who writes stupid books all day long and never goes out—or allows anyone in either—you'd damned soon try to find friends of your own age to go about with, t-try to find some amusement and you'd end by getting mixed up with the wrong sort and into a mess just like Angie has."

# Chapter 6

"There. That's the last signature. The last. I think we may say that concludes everything. Yes, that finishes it. For the moment at all events." Hubert Trefold Morton, solicitor, alderman and Mayor-expectant of Brettenden, sat back and beamed. "Probate shouldn't be long delayed. Not long. A perfectly straightforward estate. No bequests, other than the small one to Mr. and Mrs. Bloomer. Shall we say three months at the most. Your cousin was a wonderful woman. Wonderful. She did me the honour to leave her affairs entirely in my hands and I flatter myself I didn't do too badly by her. Not too badly at all. Of course, placed as I am with my knowledge of local affairs, I have my finger on the pulse so to speak and when there's just that extra little bit of capital lying around, I'm in a position to know when is a mortgage not a mortgage, as one might say." He laughed lustily. "Property. That's the thing. When you own land you own it, I maintain. And while we're on the subject of property, Sweetbriars itself is a very nice little place. Very nice indeed. I don't know whether you intend to live there, or are considering selling."

"I've not made up my mind," murmured Miss Seeton.

"No, no, quite. Early days yet. Early days. If you should consider it, remember we could probably do a very satisfactory deal there. Very satisfactory in fact." He beamed again. "Now, is there anything you wanted to know? Any little point on which I can be of assistance?"

Miss Seeton pressed her fingertips to her forehead. "No, nothing that I can think of, thank you." Really, this Mr. Morton, so overpowering, though she was sure he meant to be very helpful and kind, did boom at one so. She didn't know how cousin Flora ... But then, of course, and certainly latterly, most business would have been transacted by correspondence and at least letters didn't make a noise. She sighed and stood up.

Mr. Trefold Morton came ponderously to his feet and leaned on the desk. "I hope you don't mind my saying so, Miss Seeton, and with no wish to be ungallant, you seem a little tired. Not quite the thing, you know. Not the thing at all. Of course it's not to be wondered at, from what one reads in the papers you've been having a most distressing time. Very distressing. And there's a rumour—only just a rumour, but you know how these things get about in small communities and, after all, Plummergen's not so far away, not far—there was another distressing incident last night. Of course I don't believe half I hear. Very little of what I hear, in fact. But they say there were shots ..." He paused expectantly.

Miss Seeton collected her things. She couldn't—no, she really couldn't—go into all that.

Mr. Trefold Morton passed off his disappointment. "All wildly exaggerated, I've no doubt. No doubt at all. But none the less tiring. You must take more care of yourself. After a certain age we all have to take that little extra care. Would you like me to call the garage and order a car to take you home?"

"No, please. It's quite unnecessary." Miss Seeton was firm. The thought of having to wait for a car while this Mr. Morton continued to boom at her was unendurable. Also he seemed to say most things at least twice, as if one was slow of understanding. But then he was on the council and she believed he did quite a lot of public speaking; that probably accounted for it. "I'm perfectly all right," she assured him, "it's only that I have a rather bad headache. But I'm sure that a little fresh air will soon put it right."

"A headache?" Mr. Trefold Morton looked at her sharply. "Come, we can't have that. Oh, no. We certainly can't have that." He picked up a pen and began jotting down some figures on a pad. He did some quick calculations and, apparently satisfied with the result, crumpled up the sheet and threw it in the wastepaper-basket. "Wait here a moment. I think I have just the thing for you. Unless I gave them away, that is. But I don't think—no, I'm sure I didn't. They'd be just the very thing." He opened a door behind him and hurried out.

The office contracted into a grateful silence; the furniture shrank to normal proportions; the air and Miss Seeton's head ceased to vibrate. Not for long. Ebullience returned with Mr. Trefold Morton holding up in triumph a small phial of pills.

"Eureka, dear lady, here we are. When you get home, lie down and take one of these. Miraculous you'll find them. Miraculous."

"It's very kind of you, Mr. Morton …"

He winced. "Trefold Morton. We use the full name."

"… Mr. Trefold Morton, but I seldom take drugs."

"Drugs?" He swelled. "Good heavens, no. Nothing of the kind I assure you. Homoeopathic, I believe. They were given me by a friend. A dear friend. Some time ago. When things were—er—a little difficult. They did wonders for me. Wonders. Now, not another word." He pressed the phial into her hand. "Don't forget. Take one as soon as you get home. And take one again whenever you find the strain too much, with this trying time you're having. Tremendously relaxing you'll find them. Tremendously."

Disgraceful. Truly scandalous—those two women in front. And at the top of their voices, too. Should she interfere, wondered Miss Seeton? Tell them there wasn't a word of truth in what they were saying. But it would be so embarrassing to make a scene. And in a bus, too. Somehow that made it worse. Anywhere else you could say what you thought and walk away. But you couldn't walk away in a bus, at least not far. Unless you stopped it and got off. Then, of course, you would have to walk—rather too far. Or wait two hours for the next one. Oh dear, she wished she had agreed to Mr. Trefold Morton's suggestion of a car to take her home. Miss Seeton sat and seethed. The woman on the other side from them had called the fat one Mrs. Blaine. So the thin one must be Miss Nuttel. Nigel had been quite right about them. Dreadful women. To dare to say that Miss Venning had attacked her last night. And that she, of all people, had tried to shoot the girl. How on earth did they dream up such fantastic ideas? Just because some silly boy tried to steal some eggs. To drag Miss Venning's name into it was monstrous.

The bus slowed and stopped to pick up a plump, fresh-faced little woman, standing at the side of the road at an opening where a lane wandered quietly between hedgerows. The white painted sign pointing down the lane was lettered in black The Meadows.

Miss Seeton rose and hurried down the aisle. She'd remembered: this must be where the Vennings lived. They weren't far from Plummergen now, only about a mile. She could perfectly well walk back from here. How very fortunate that she'd noticed. She'd go at once and explain. Apologise. She'd scotch this mischievous rumour before it had time to do any damage. She swept past Miss Nuttel and Mrs. Blaine without a glance and the plump little woman stepped aside to make room as she descended.

Mrs. Fratters looked back in surprise as she climbed aboard the bus. Someone calling on Madam. That wouldn't go down well. But it couldn't be helped. She hadn't time now to go trapesing after her to find out what she wanted. She'd never get back in time for lunch with the Kenya Continental. And if Madam had to go without her coffee, that wouldn't go down well either. They'd had quite enough to-dos for one morning with Miss Angie in the state she was in.

The Nuts watched Miss Seeton's hurrying figure and exchanged pregnant glances. The bus started; drew away. Through the open window floated a bright titter and the words: "What did I tell you? If ever proof was needed …"

Miss Seeton's wave of indignation carried her crest-high until she was half-way down the lane, then treacherously receded, leaving her to flounder in cross-currents of doubt.

She'd had no idea that Mrs. Venning lived so far out. So—so isolated. It was quite possible, in fact now she thought of it, even probable, that Mrs. Venning might not have heard of this dreadful rumour. Or at all events not yet. It was one thing to deplore malicious scandal and reassure an innocent victim, but it was quite another thing if the victim didn't know she was a victim—or in this case should it be, perhaps, they were victims—and one had to explain what it was one was deploring before one could deplore it. To reassure someone who didn't know that they needed reassurance would mean that one would have to make it clear oneself what the reason for reassurance was and why the need to ... oh, dear, how complicated. And, of course, embarrassing. On the other hand, if Mrs. Venning and her daughter knew nothing as yet of what was being said, surely it would be better—kinder, for they were bound to learn of it in time—to forewarn them. To, so to speak, remove the poison from the sting before it stung. In which case it was one's clear duty. But then again, bearers of bad tidings. There were too many ways of looking at it.

Looking at it from every conceivable angle, Miss Seeton went forward on doubtful feet. Facing her was a high brick wall, partially covered with evergreen honeysuckle and variegated ivies. The lane turned sharp right; running alongside the wall and ending at large wooden gates, with a small door to one side. Miss Seeton approached the door.

It was all rather intimidating. One half expected a sentry on guard. There was no bell, no knocker, no letter-box even. Just a plain wooden door with a ring-handled latch. She opened the door and went through. The effect was strange. She hadn't realised there was quite a wind today, until it was cut off as she closed the door behind her. Such peace. No, peace wasn't the right word. Stillness. If one were fanciful one might almost say a brooding stillness.

On her right was a courtyard and a garage. On her left, an attractively blended shrub border. In front of her a concrete path ran to the back of a small out-house of some kind. To its right, a glasshouse; to its left the path curved out of sight behind a high clipped hedge.

No one about. No sound. Rounding the curve she was faced with—yes, it must be—the back of the house. The steep tiled roof sloped down to a low oak door. A miniature ship's bell hung near the door which, like the windows on either side, was closed. But a latch window farther on was ajar; the nearest to a sign of life she'd seen. Did one ring the bell? Should one go round to the front? It was so difficult to know what was right. Many people in these old houses used the back door all the time. Perhaps it would be more correct to go round.

The front door was of plain oak with a heavy wooden drawlatch. No bell. No knocker. No letter-box. What did the postman do, she wondered? She tapped on the door with the handle of her umbrella. There was a period of silence, broken abruptly by the rattle of the bolts being drawn. The latch lifted and the door swung outward, forcing Miss Seeton to step back. A tall woman with a handsome haunted face looked at her in silent inquiry. Unnerved, Miss Seeton flustered.

"Oh dear. Have I come to the wrong door?"

"Yes."

Miss Seeton fled. The bolts clanged back into their sockets. Mrs. Venning walked through the house, Miss Seeton hurried round it, to arrive breathless at the back door as it opened and she faced the same situation, the same woman, the same look, the same silence.

It was ridiculous to let oneself be agitated by a little thing like going to the wrong door. After all, it was a very natural mistake and obviously Mrs. Venning thought so too, or she wouldn't have come straight to this one and opened it ready, as she had. But, somehow, it did make it even more difficult to explain why she'd called. How to put it? Really, the best thing would be to state the facts quite simply. Let them speak for themselves.

"I really came to apologise," she began. "Well, not to apologise exactly—at least not in that sense—for, of course, it was nothing that I'd done, myself. Only I was so very, very shocked to hear it. And, as I of all people knew there wasn't a word of truth in it and as I happened to be passing by your lane, I thought it only right to make that quite clear straight away."

Sonia Venning regarded her visitor. Finally: "I haven't the remotest idea what you're talking about."

Miss Seeton looked worried. "You are Mrs. Venning?"

"I am."

Miss Seeton smiled with relief. "That's all right, then. It was foolish of me, I should have asked that in the first place. I quite understand your not understanding what I'm talking about. I did realise that was very possible, but on thinking it over I felt it was essential that you should be put in possession of the facts, so that you could ignore it or refute it when you did hear, as you'd be bound to eventually."

"What are you talking about?"

"Eggs," Miss Seeton told her earnestly. "They said that your daughter had stolen my eggs. It's outrageous."

Mrs. Venning was calm, her voice acid. "Who said this?"

"A Mrs. Blaine, I think their names are, and a Miss Nuttel."

"Then I don't think we need let it disturb either of us. They'd say anything."

"But it was on a bus, in public."

"Angela is supposed to have stolen your eggs on a bus? It's too puerile to bother with."

"No. You don't understand. It was said on a bus. Everybody could hear. I thought of protesting, but I'm afraid I couldn't bring myself to make a public scene. And then I saw your signboard, so I got off and came straight here. What actually happened last night was just childish and silly. But with the shooting, and then the police becoming involved, the whole thing could easily become a scandal. And to bring your daughter's name into it, wantonly like that, is unforgivable."

Mrs. Venning's face was an expressionless mask. She moved aside. "I think you'd better come in and clarify this absurdity."

Sonia Venning considered her visitor; considered her story. Certainly it wasn't true. What was less certain was how much truth the story contained. No village boy would have gone searching for eggs after midnight. Conceivable, but unlikely, that he might have been after the birds themselves. Inconceivable that he should have been armed. The various members of the Colveden family appeared so promptly in their cues, that one was tempted to suspect that the cues were pre-arranged. All this must be connected with the police action last night of which she'd heard from Mrs. Fratters who, in turn, had got her information from the milkman. Not just the local bobby at that, but mobile police in cars. More than one car. Was there a trap here? Or was this woman telling the truth so far as she knew it? Angela had arrived home soon after midnight. And alone. But it was easy to see

102

how the village would link her with the affair. And, in point of fact, they were probably right. The essence being, how far was Angela involved this time? And could it be proved? On the whole, she decided, Miss Seeton was genuine, with this story of some pot of jam that they were supposed to have left on her. Well, maybe Angela had. This female was presumably giving the facts as she knew them and activated solely by a desire to help. She rose.

"You've been more than kind in coming here and I'm extremely grateful. I know how inaccurate and malicious village gossip can be. Or any gossip, for that matter. But it's always better to be forewarned. I'm sorry if I seemed a little abrupt when you first arrived, but my housekeeper is out shopping and I was working"—she gestured towards the typewriter and the litter of papers on the desk— "and one gets immersed. It's so difficult to switch one's concentration. Particularly," she smiled apologetically, and put her hand to her head, "when one has an extremely bad headache."

"I'm so sorry. How dreadful for you," sympathised Miss Seeton. "Shouldn't you lie down? But what a curious coincidence." She opened her bag and began to hunt in it. "I was given something for a headache only this morning. It's in here somewhere. I'm most unlikely to use them as I don't care for taking drugs myself."

"Why not? Who's not caring about taking drugs?"

Both women turned at the interruption. Mrs. Venning went quickly to the door.

"Angela, what are you doing down here? Go back to your room."

"Oh, don't be so fud. What gives? What's that old … ?"

"Don't argue with me. Go back to your room at once. You aren't well. You weren't well last night, if you remember. Go back to bed and stay there as I told you or I shall have you seriously ill. It could easily be serious, do you understand. Now, will you do as I say." Reluctantly her daughter retreated up the stairs. A door slammed. Mrs. Venning forced a smile. "I'm so sorry ..."

"Please." Miss Seeton was distressed. "It is I who am sorry. Such a worry for you. And the young—so impatient. Always sure that they know best. Now what was I ... ? Oh yes, of course. I don't know if they'll be any good to you, but I'm told they're excellent." From her handbag she brought the phial of pills. "These, for your headache. Do try them if you think they'll be any help."

The smile froze on Sonia Venning's face. She gave a high-pitched, ugly laugh. Miss Seeton recoiled. Mrs. Venning stepped forward and slapped the phial out of her hand.

"Get out," she flung at her visitor. "Get out, you lying, filthy little spy. Go on, get out. If you want money, try some other game. You've made a bad mistake this time. Go on. Go on, get out."

Lunch at Rytham Hall, for which Miss Seeton, having misjudged either the distance or her walking speed, was late, was not a success. With a guest who appeared abstracted, a son who was sullen and preoccupied and a husband who was never a brilliant conversationalist, Lady Colveden's efforts to enliven the proceedings gradually petered out and they finished the meal in silence.

After lunch Miss Seeton announced her intention of going back to her cottage. The superintendent, arriving with his sergeant to interview her, joined his arguments to the protests of the Colveden family in an attempt to dissuade her, but she stuck to her decision. Grateful as she was for shelter the previous night, she could see no reason to remain. Simply, she had fallen in love with her cottage and wanted to return. So Delphick and Bob Ranger drove her back, to conduct the interview in her own home.

Miss Seeton and the superintendent were at their ease on either side of the fireplace, while the sergeant, with his inevitable notebook, sat at a table near the front window looking on to The Street.

"So we must accept that this time the sound was working, but the vision was switched off. Or rather the lighting was faulty."

Miss Seeton smiled. "I'm afraid so, superintendent. But I think that you could be wrong in imagining it was the same boy as in London. This one was completely English."

"Lebel's parents may have been French, but he was born and bred in London, he's got no foreign accent. What was this man's voice like?"

She thought. "No. I can't help you, I'm afraid. It was just a voice. Very ordinary. Not well educated. I remember he called me 'Lady'. He said 'Go back to the house, lady'—or something like that."

"Did you see him walk at all?"

"Yes, he came forward when I first got there—to the hen-house, that is."

"Then can you remember if he limped at all? Sir George thought he did. I wondered if he genuinely has a limp, or whether he might have ricked his ankle getting away."

"Oh." There was a pause. A flush stained Miss Seeton's cheeks.

"You don't remember?" he prompted.

"Well—yes. I'm afraid I do. I feel very guilty about it. You see I was worried on account of the hens, knowing that Stan would be upset. I felt responsible. So I told him to stop—stop upsetting the hens, I mean. When he defied me and told me to go back to the house and pointed that gun at me, I'm afraid I lost all patience and smacked his wrist. And the thing exploded. I think it must have damaged his foot. I did ask him if he was hurt, but he didn't say. He only cried out and hopped about, holding his foot, before he scrambled up on to the hen-house roof and disappeared."

This was beyond. This was way, way over the odds. The sergeant was impelled to speak. He addressed his superior: "She-hee-hee!" he tittered. Shocked at the sound and wilting under The Oracle's quelling eye, he clenched his teeth. Through tight and trembling lips he said: "I'm sorry, ma'am. For the record, was it your umbrella you smacked him with?"

"Why, yes," agreed Miss Seeton. "How did you know?"

"B-Because it had to b-be. Only you—hoo-hoo …" Heroically he silenced himself by biting his tongue—hard.

"If you've quite recovered, Sergeant?"

Bob's glowing face gazed at The Oracle in mute appeal. Between pain and suppression, water welled in his eyes. Two large tears ran down his cheeks. Hastily Delphick looked away. One tear splashed on the notebook, made a blot, to remain in testimony to the emotion of the interview.

"Well … yes." Delphick had the rare experience of finding himself at a loss. He reversed his gambit and tried again. "Yes … well, that disposes of his limp. And very nice marksmanship too, if I may say so." He drew a deep breath. "Now, two other matters." He smiled. "Poor Miss Seeton,

106

it must seem to you like one unending catechism. But I'm afraid police work consists of information. Volumes of information. All of which has to be filed, tabulated, correlated and what-have-you. And from this process, if we're lucky, emerge facts. Information is occasionally given to us, but mostly we go out and dig for it—with endless questions."

"But of course, Superintendent. I'm only too willing to help, if I can. I don't see how you can do your work if people don't tell you things."

"Right. Now, there's an authoress, living locally, who writes what some people refer to as 'stupid' books."

"You mean Mrs. Venning? I don't know about stupid. I believe her books are very successful. I've never read any myself. They're books for small children."

"And she has a daughter called Angie."

"Angela, yes."

"Have you met them?"

"Yes."

Give him credit, thought the sergeant. Hadn't been able to find out the name of young Colveden's 'stupid authoress' at lunch-time because the local P.C. was out on his beat, he'd now winkled the information out of Miss Seeton without her even knowing she'd given it. He'd be asking for a description next.

"What are they like?" asked Delphick.

"I'm sorry—I can't say. I've only spoken to Mrs. Venning once. And I haven't met her daughter, only saw her. She wasn't at all well."

"But you must have formed some impression—of the mother, at least. What kind of woman is she?"

She baulked. "I—I don't know, Superintendent, I can't tell you."

"Then tell me, how did you happen to meet her? I understood she was something of a recluse."

"I called on her."

"Recently?"

"Yes. This morning, on my way back. Just before lunch. I'd overheard something spiteful and, knowing it was quite untrue, I thought she should be warned. So I called on her and ..."

"And?"

"And ..." She faltered again. Her hands moved restlessly. "And that's all."

"I'm sorry to badger you, but it is important for me to learn more of the Vennings. If you remember, you agreed we couldn't do our work if people didn't tell us things."

"It isn't that I won't—it's that I can't. Oh, I could tell you that she was a little strange in her behaviour. And that she was very rude to me. But it would be wrong, don't you see. It wouldn't be the truth." Again the uncharacteristic restlessness of the hands. "Not the real truth."

Delphick had been watching her intently. He jumped to his feet. "Got it. Off you go. Find yourself paper, your drawing-block, pencils, paints, whatever it is you need. The sergeant and I will take a turn round the garden, if we may. We'll examine the chicken houses, the wall, the ground beyond it. We'll crawl about on our hands and knees and spoil our trousers. We'll observe blades of grass through magnifying glasses. Have you got your magnifying glass, sergeant?"

"No, sir."

"Good. Then we'll use the eyes our National Health has given us and see sweet nothing at all. But at least we shall look like sleuths. While you stay here and do some paper work." He swung round on her with a broad smile. "I'm right, aren't I? That's how you resolve your problems, find out about people, get at the truth—your fingers tell you, don't they? You put it down on paper and then you can see it—then you know? Am I right?"

Miss Seeton was acutely embarrassed. "I don't think … well, perhaps. Yes—in a way, I mean—it's true I do draw things. And people. I always feel one shouldn't. But I can't help myself, somehow. It's—it's compulsive really. But it does help—help me, that is—to see things more clearly. But, of course, they're quite private. Rather, in a way I suppose, like a very private diary. I never let anyone else see them."

"Except us. We're the confessional, remember. We're doctors, priests; we're that anomalous anodyne for society's ills, detectives. To think that I nearly didn't recognise a drug-taker's craving because it happened to be paper and pencil, not pills. I ought to be put out to grass." He grinned at her. "We'll leave you to it. Come along, Sergeant, grass it shall be."

Miss Seeton watched them go through the french windows and down the garden. What an understanding man the superintendent was, very comforting somehow. And that enormous young man with the notebook, who so rarely spoke. They were both—dependable, that was it. She sat at the writing-desk near the window, pulled open one of the long drawers and took some cartridge paper from her portfolio, collected pencils, charcoal and erasers, shut the drawer, pulled down the flap and spread out her things. For a few moments she enjoyed the air from the open window, the view of the garden and the quiet. How pleasant it was. How lucky she'd been. She turned back to the writing-desk, to find that her hand, of its own volition, had taken up a piece of charcoal and had started blocking in. Mindlessly at first, then with increasing concentration, Miss Seeton began to give vent to her feelings.

The hens, who had shown a slight interest on the detectives' arrival, now, since no food had been forthcoming, ignored them. Bob clambered back and sat astride the wall.

"Were you expecting to find anything down here, sir?"

"Such as a few packets of heroin wot slipped out of 'is 'and while 'e was scarperin'?" The Oracle grinned amiably. "No, Bob. And if he dropped a few in on the chickens, I'm all for letting sleeping birds lie. Who am I to interfere with their simple pleasures. And I don't think we can have you searching the hen-houses, for even if we could get you inside, if you let your breath out, or had another fit of hysterics, you'd blow the whole structure down."

Bob was abashed. "I'm awfully sorry about that, sir— laughing. I just couldn't help myself."

"Forget it. But another time, if you must cry, have the decency not to look at me during the performance. That was almost my undoing."

"You. You never batted an eyelid, sir."

"I'm delighted to hear it, but I should hate to guarantee that I haven't ruptured something rather serious inside. All we're doing down here at the moment is filling in time and going through the motions, in case there's anything to see. It's a pity that back wall's so low," he reflected, "it probably improves the view from the house, but at that height it's a positive invitation to the dance."

110

"Do you think Lebel's got contacts down here, sir?"

"Not accomplices in the sense you mean it, no. But people he could contact, yes. You must remember, Bob, that drugs mean big money and big money means big organisation. I should imagine that Lebel's no more than a small-time runner and hatchet-man for them, but an organisation, if it wants to run smoothly, must protect its own people, or eliminate them. At the moment Miss Seeton is inconvenient to them because she can put the finger on someone who is evidently useful to them, but if we can catch up with him, or make things sufficiently hot that he becomes an inconvenience, with any luck they'll kill him and leave her alone which, though it may not please the drug squad, will save us a lot of leg-work."

"And you think Mrs. Venning is mixed up in it, sir?"

"Entangled in the fringe, I should guess."

"It seems odd for someone like her. She's quite well known."

"Don't tell me you're a fan?"

"My sister's kids—they love her books. They're all about a character called Jack the Rabbit."

"Such erudition," said Delphick admiringly. "Well, it's possible that the mother's only covering up for the daughter, who sounds like a main-liner to me."

"You think the girl is hooked, then?"

"Merely speculating. But young Colveden has evidently been worried about her for some time. For what he didn't say, she was obviously in on the party with those young punks last night. And according to Miss Seeton, she's ill this morning. It sounds a drearily familiar pattern."

"Pity," commented Bob.

"Oh, yes," agreed Delphick. "And t'will be pittier still if 'tis true. However, cheer up, it may not be like that at all. It's ... I don't like amateurs without the weight mixing it with the professionals. It's dangerous. That's why I slapped the Colveden boy down. Making him lose his temper was the only way to get him to talk. All his running around playing peek-a-boo and I-spy, while trying to cover up for the Venning girl, could easily have landed him in hospital, or worse. And a lot she seems to care. He did a good job putting those other young disasters in the ditch, it gave us all their names and addresses on a plate, so the narcotics boys can now concentrate on them, instead of just vaguely on the club. They don't matter in themselves, it's who starts them off in the first place and who supplies them in the second. But the Vennings, I feel ..." he shrugged. "I don't know; I'm not happy about it. Come on. Perhaps Miss Seeton can give us a clue. She's had time to fill Burlington House by now."

"I don't see what you expect to get, sir, by her trying to draw Mrs. Venning. After all she's not likely to stick her behind bars, like she did Lebel."

"It would be highly informative if she did. I'm not sure what I expect, but I've a shrewd suspicion that woman's psychic, without knowing it. But whether, by drawing the subject, it will clarify her mind and she'll be able to tell us what she thinks, or whether there'll be something helpful in the drawing itself, I can't even guess. Come on, let's go and find out."

As they approached the french windows they could see Miss Seeton was absorbed. She was working with charcoal, smudging and shading with thumb, fingers and bits of cotton wool. They stood to one side and watched. After a few moments she sat back and studied what she'd been doing, then took a piece of charcoal and scrubbed it across the top of the paper, working it in with the heel of her hand. She pushed away her chair, got up and surveyed the result. Delphick moved forward.

"May we come in?"

She turned, startled, looked at them blankly, then, coming back to earth: "Oh, Superintendent. Yes, of course, come in. I was just going to clean myself up. Charcoal's such a messy medium." She held out two grimy hands; she had managed to get smears on her face as well. "I won't be a moment."

They stood contemplating the littered desk. On top was the charcoal drawing on which they had seen her at work. Well, you couldn't win every time, reflected the sergeant. The Oracle had fallen down on this one. Or rather Miss Seeton had. They'd been trotting round the garden, while she was supposed to be running off a few front and side views of the Venning family. Only she'd forgotten all about it and settled down to a bit of landscaping. Pretty gloomy at that. Clever enough, he supposed, but he wouldn't want to live with it. All those mountains at the back, with that dark sky on top. It was—brooding. Yes, that was the word, brooding. And that cliff on the left—no, not a cliff exactly—a rock. Just that one ray of light catching the stream as it trickled down—there were two streams actually, but one disappeared over the other side—lighting up the pool at the bottom where—good Lord!—some girl had come a purler and dropped a bottle or something that had smashed. He wouldn't give much for the girl's chances. She looked as if she was lying half in the water. Bit ominous, the whole thing. Not his cup of tea at all. Delphick pulled a sheet of paper from underneath the drawing. Bob chuckled. This was more like it. This was something you could understand. It was a quick pen sketch, done in a few lines. On a rostrum, behind a table above which was festooned a mayoral chain in place of bunting, a portly, pompous figure was delivering a speech while holding up a phial in his right hand: a wicked likeness to Mr. Trefold Morton in the role of a huckster selling quack medicines.

"Who," laughed Delphick as Miss Seeton returned, "is the gentleman you don't like?"

"Oh," exclaimed Miss Seeton. "You weren't supposed to see that." She looked at him reprovingly. "It was underneath."

"I know," agreed Delphick, "but the corner was sticking out and I couldn't resist it. It's very funny."

"It was naughty of me, I admit. But he did boom so. It's my cousin's solicitor. I had to see him this morning about probate and he would insist on giving me pills for a headache. I didn't want them, but it was easier to take them than argue."

The superintendent considered: it certainly was funny. And yet ... A con man if ever he'd seen one. And the odd coincidence of a bottle or phial in both drawings. Coincidence? A little probing there might pay off. A few inquiries into this man's financial standing and that of his clients ... But with a solicitor any such investigation would need to be discreet.

He put the sketch down and regarded the charcoal drawing. Miss Seeton watched him anxiously. "I don't know that it's very clear. Does it help at all?"

"Oh, yes. I think so." The sergeant glanced at him in surprise. "I'm not too happy about it—or the implications. But, oh yes, I think it helps. 'Like Niobe all tears.'"

She glowed with pleasure. "Then you do understand how I felt."

"You say she was rude to you?"

"Well, yes—in a way. But I'm sure it was a misunderstanding. She had a headache and I offered her Mr. Trefold Morton's pills. She knocked them out of my hand and said something about spying and told me to get out. But I'm sure she didn't mean it. It's just that I think she's very unhappy and on edge."

Delphick pointed to the picture. "Hence the broken bottle down here?"

She nodded. "You see, I'd interrupted Mrs. Venning in the middle of working and creative people don't like that. It's very understandable."

"What's worrying you, Sergeant?"

Bob was looking perplexed. "It's that I don't get this Niobe business, sir. I know the statue and I thought she was a Greek lady who couldn't stop crying because all her children were dead."

"A Greek myth," corrected The Oracle. "Artemis and her brother killed all Niobe's children except one daughter and turned Niobe herself into a rock and her tears became twin streams that ran from it. The rock, Sergeant. Can't you see the woman's face in it?"

Suddenly Bob could. Those shadows and vegetation were the eyes, the nose, the mouth. Like a tragic mask. Couldn't think why he hadn't seen it before. Couldn't see it any other way now. All the children killed except one daughter. He looked at the bottom of the drawing again. The girl lying crumpled half in the water. He didn't like the implication either.

# Chapter 7

Really, it was very muddling. "Tread the earth well down when planting so that no air-pockets are left round the roots." That seemed clear and sensible enough. Then, a few pages later, under "Care and Attention", it said, "Fork well round the roots to let in air." Surely it seemed a pity not to have left the air there in the first place. And now it said on page fifty-three, "Never fork roses as, being suface rooters, you may damage the roots." Miss Seeton closed the book and put it on the grass beside her. *Greenfinger Points the Way.* Yes, but which way? It pointed in so many directions. Was gardening, perhaps, like some of the other professions, she wondered? One knew that, in many cases, unsuccessful singers taught singing, unsuccessful authors taught writing and, as one knew oneself only too well, unsuccessful artists taught drawing. In fact one liked to console oneself that such persons made the best teachers. And there was no question that, if one were successful, one would hardly have the time to teach. So could it be, she mused, that unsuccessful gardeners wrote gardening books? Or was that heresy? Certainly one got the impression that if one did half the things that appeared to be vital if any plant were to survive, one would have no time at all, even for meals. It really was very muddling indeed. She must ask Stan. She heard a tapping. Probably someone who had tried the front door and failed to get an answer. She got up, crossed the lawn, took the key off its nail and opened the side door in the wall.

"C'n I int'rest you in sump'n, miss?" Bright eyes gleamed under a tangle of ginger. The sinuous, eager movements of youth—appealing; the clear complexion fading, the puppy-fat receding; guileless cherub yielding to disingenuous ferret.

Miss Seeton was puzzled. "Interest me? In what?"

"Anything, miss, for gossakes. Fresh veg., bottles of pop, eggs, cheese, canned stuff. No kidd'n—you name it, we got it."

"Really, I don't think there's anything I need just at the moment, thank you."

"Aw, c'mon! Cheaper y'see, cuts out the middleman. We bring it right to your door f'you to choose. C'mon, take a look-see," he wheedled, "can't hurt you none to take a look."

Miss Seeton moved forward as he stepped to one side. Backed at right angles across the lane, the back doors open and touching the wall on either side of her, was an elderly car, the rear half converted to a van. On the floor inside were two or three cabbages in sere and yellow leaf, some bottles of ginger beer and a cardboard box out of which were sticking tins of soup and packets of detergent.

Miss Seeton regarded the disheartening array. "I'm afraid I really don't think that ..."

Her sentence finished in a muffled squawk as a sack descended over her head, her ankles were seized and she was pitched among the merchandise. The doors were slammed, a jolt as the driver jumped into his seat, a jar as he banged his door, the engine roared and Miss Seeton, accompanied by bottles, was rolled from one side to the other as the van lurched forward, backed, then sped up the lane.

Miss Seeton squirmed and writhed to free her arms; to free herself from the stifling mustiness of sacking which enveloped her. But the sway of the car made co-ordinated movement difficult. Objects with sharp or blunt edges would move in to unexpected attack. If she found something on which to gain purchase for her feet, she no sooner braced herself than that something melted to nothing and she was once more rolling helpless at large; rolling on, rolling off, endless bottles—surely there hadn't been so many. On one of these excursions something jabbed her painfully in the neck, catching the sack, holding it. She wriggled downward, freed her elbows. Now it was simple. She pushed the sack over her head and sat up in the dark to take stock of her position, drawing grateful breaths of stale cabbage and petrol; ozone after her enmuzzlement. Miss Seeton, rarely angry on her own behalf, was cross.

This was beyond a joke. It was outrageous. Perhaps that redheaded boy was the one who'd been after the eggs and this was his idea of revenge. He probably thought it was a lark. But it wasn't funny. Not in the least. A perfectly good hat, and almost new—it must be ruined. Leaning back against the side of the van she put up tentative hands. Yes, she'd thought so—squashed. Her indignation rose. It was no good knocking, calling him to stop. If he'd intended to stop he'd never have started. Where were they going? And what did he imagine he could do when they got there? Really, the

118

young—so thoughtless. Never considering the consequences. No, she must shift for herself. But how? How did you stop a car when you were shut up in the back of it?

Patting and feeling, she began to crawl about the floor. At one side something jutted up with what felt like a large rubber cap. She clung to it for support as the car heeled round a corner. The cap came away in her hand and she fell backwards. The reek of petrol grew overpowering. Miss Seeton crept back to its source.

Yes, there was a slopping sound down there. If only one could see. It was so difficult trying to guess in the dark. Really, the smell was quite awful. But how odd. Of course she knew nothing about cars, but surely the petrol was usually on the outside. Perhaps vans were different. She put out her hand to replace the cap. No—wait. Something ... Now what was it? Yes. Water in the petrol. She'd heard people complain of that. "It wouldn't go because water had got into the petrol." Water. Well, she hadn't any. But—remembering—would ginger beer do? She began to search. The bottles, so obtrusive earlier in her predicament, now proved elusive. At last. Here was one. Two more, as if attracted by the capture of their friend, rolled bumping against her legs. She gathered them up and prepared for action. How fortunate, they had screw stoppers. She poured all three down the pipe that stuck through the floor. Apparently wanting to join the game, a cardboard box nudged her. She pushed it away. Oh—one moment. Wasn't there ... ? Yes, packets of detergent poking from that box. Would they help? She pulled one out and started to tear the top. How ... curious. She'd never known ... such tough cardboard. There. That should do. Fumbling a little, she tipped the contents down the pipe. Satisfied that she had done all she could, she pushed the rubber cap back into place, hoping to lessen the stench that was making her head reel. At least, she reflected, with all this shaking, it should foam up nicely down there. The van rattled on its way. No good … it hadn't worked. Dizzying clouds, held at bay by action, began to engulf her mind. The van gave a polite hiccup. Could that be … ? No, they were still moving. Two more hiccups. Miss Seeton tried to take an interest. A series of hiccups. Very tiring, thought Miss Seeton dreamily—and could prove dangerous if prolonged. People had died of hiccups. Silence descended as the engine cut out and they coasted, swaying, to a stop.

"In trouble, mate?"

A ginger mop withdrew from under the bonnet, leaving its useless scrutiny and ineffectual fiddling. "Dunno. Guess it's sump'n in the pump. Plenty of gas but not getting through." He eyed the burly driver of a light blue van which had drawn up just beyond him. "Guess you needn't worry none. Soon have it right."

"Not that way you won't. Here, give us that spanner." Faint tapping sounded from the back. "What you carting, mate, livestock?"

"No, dad. Just bits 'n pieces and one old hen t' deliver."

The burly man undid the nut to the petrol feed. "Now we'll soon see." They did. Out spumed a froth of blue bubbles. "What you runnin' on, mate, soapsuds?" He threw back his head and roared with laughter.

"Help!" sounded faintly from within the van. His laugh cut off. He turned. A click. He swung back only half prepared for the attack. The knife ripped into his left arm instead of his stomach. His boot came up; contacted. His assailant screeched; bent double. His right fist came down and it was over. Catching hold of a foot he dragged the unconscious boy to his own van, reached in, took twine, bound the body and threw it to one side. He strode to the back of the other car, twisted the bar handle and flung open the doors. He gaped.

"Strewth, miss. Take it easy."

He held out his hand. Head swimming and gulping fresh air, Miss Seeton pulled herself forward and managed to alight. She stood on precarious feet to thank her rescuer, but her knees buckled and she knelt before her salvation.

"So sorry," she murmured vaguely. "The fumes, you know. So strong."

He lifted her up and held her. "Easy now, miss. Feel swimmy enough I doubt, cooped up in there."

She gasped. "Your arm. You're hurt."

He glanced down. Blood was dripping from his hand and seeping through his coat sleeve. "It's nothing, miss. Just a jab from your chauffeur there."

"You mean he actually attacked you? He must be out of his mind. I'm most dreadfully sorry. And grateful, too. I don't know how to thank you. I don't know what I should have done. What happened? Did he run away?"

"Not to say run, he's back there sleeping it off. I tied him up neat enough so he'll not come to no harm."

Miss Seeton was recovering. "Take that coat off," she ordered, "and let me see your arm at once."

The wound upon examination proved less serious than she had feared. She made a pad with a clean handkerchief from her pocket and bound it tightly with a moderately clean one from his. The burly man watched her with interest.

"I've got it. You're the lady in the papers, aren't you, miss? The one they call 'The Battling Brolly'. There was a picture of you. What you been up to this time? Chasing our ginger friend?" With quickening interest: "Is he the one that did that girl in London?"

"No, no, he's not. There's no connection—at least I don't think so." She looked doubtful. "I can only imagine it's a silly—well—joke, I suppose. Somebody tried to steal some eggs the other night. I woke up and managed to stop him. And either it was he, it was too dark for me to be sure, or it's one of his friends trying to get back at me."

The burly man looked doubtful. "If you say so, miss. What do we do now? We can't leave young Ginger lying about. Can't leave the van neither. I'll allow there's not much traffic this way. But it's narrow enough for passing. We'd best sling him in the back. I'll give you a tow."

"Tow?" She was disturbed. "Oh, I don't think I could. I've never driven a car."

"And you won't be driving this one neither. Nor no one else. Don't know what he filled her up with but it's coming out blue bubbles."

"I poured something down a pipe where the petrol seemed to be, hoping that might stop it. It was the only thing I could think of to do," she explained.

"It did that sure enough." He peered into the back, saw the bottles and let out a whoop of laughter. "Our Ginger stoned by Stone Ginger. That's rich enough, that is." Chuckling and delighted with his wit, he went to his own van, backed it up and returned with a length of rope. He began to tie the two vehicles together.

Miss Seeton joined him. Looking down at the trussed body, "Is he all right?" she asked tentatively.

"Right enough, miss. Should be waking up soon, or thereabouts. I doubt he'll have a stiff neck and a sore— well, he won't walk none too easy for a day or two. Do him good."

She picked up the knife. "What about this? We oughtn't to leave it here, do you think?"

"You're right, better give it me." Miss Seeton wiped off the blood as best she could on the grass and handed it over. "I'll turn it in to the police along with him."

"The police?" she exclaimed. "Oh, must we? No, no, of course you're right," she agreed, seeing his expression, "I do realise that. To attack you with a knife—quite unforgivable. It was just … I hadn't thought. So stupid of me. But the police—and then the newspapers. They're sure to think—to imagine … Oh dear, how very tiresome!"

The burly man stood up with a satisfied grunt. "There we are, miss, that should hold. Now we'll just get rid of Carrot-top here." He scooped up the body which was beginning to stir. "Starting to take an interest in things, is he? Well, it's time enough he was out of the way. I doubt he'll have a few things to say when he comes round which saving your presence wouldn't be fitting." He tossed the body into the back of its own van, closed the doors and turned the handle to lock them. "Come on, miss, in you get."

Miss Seeton viewed the prospect with alarm. Nervousness made her voluble. "Of course, I do see that you're right, about not leaving his van here, I mean, on such a narrow road, particularly with him inside it, I mean, if there was an accident, he might be hurt and do you feel up to driving with your bad arm?"

"It's right enough, miss. Can't feel it but it'll do."

"I can't think it wise for me to try and steer, you see, I don't know how."

"Nothing to it, miss. Come along I'll show you." Miss Seeton got in and sat upright, apprehensive. He placed her hands on the steering-wheel. "Now, remember, right hand down you go right. Left hand down you go left." She followed his instructions. "That's it, miss, but don't grip so tight. Take it easy. And this," he put her foot on a pedal, "is the brake. Keep your foot on it but not hard and press it when you want to slow. Aim to keep the rope tight between us. Only push the pedal right down if you want to stop. But don't do it sudden or you may snap the tow. Don't worry. I'll be keeping an eye on you in the mirror. And we'll take it slow and easy. Straight along here," he pointed ahead, "joins the Brettenden road. We turn left there. Then it's dead straight except for the bends." He closed her door, grinned at her, gave her a thumbs-up and jumped into his own van. Gently, hesitatingly, they began to fluctuate down the road.

Why couldn't witnesses use their eyes, despaired Delphick. Two women, from cottages opposite, who had seen a van in the lane by Miss Seeton's side-door had described the driver as tall, short, fair, red-haired, young and couldn't-say-I'm-sure. And another woman, shopping in The Street, remembered a strange van passing at approximately the right time driven by a "dreadful-looking man with a white face and gleaming eyes." The best description of the van, was that it was low; dark brown or black. The only certainty was that the man had headed north from Plummergen. It was such long odds, he thought, as the sergeant put the car into gear for their fifth sedate patrol of the Brettenden road. These endless side roads. Nothing more they could have done. Road blocks to all main roads. All available motor-cycle patrols out. He envied young Colveden rushing round scouring the countryside in that M.G. He almost envied Sir George lumbering about in a vast utility that looked like a trippers' coach. They'd get this man in time of course— bound to. But that wouldn't be in time … And catching him later, what proof would they have? Unless by a lucky fluke there were some clues left in the van. And that would prove too late to be lucky for her.

They pulled off the road at the double bend on the rise just above the spot where Nigel had ditched the car from The Singing Swan and looked down over the marsh. In the distance two vans, one hard on the wheels of the other, crawled from a side road and turned left towards Brettenden.

They alerted. The rear van was low. And dark. From here it could be either grey or brown. Delphick switched to transmission.

"Car 403. Car 403. Position: mile north of Plummergen, proceeding Brettenden. Two vans half-mile ahead, approx., turned from side road, proceeding Brettenden. Slow pace, leading van large, colour light blue. Rear van low, colour dark grey or brown." Bob got under way again as Delphick's voice quickened. "Rear van driving dangerously. All over the road, pulling out to pass on bend. Swinging back … Trying again." His voice rose. "Car coming towards them—they'll crash. No … they're swinging back. Still trying … fighting to pass. Dangerous driving—could be quarry. Am giving chase. Over."

He looked at her. He turned his back on Bob's beaming face as the sergeant settled into the driving seat of the converted van to take over the tow. He looked at her. All his distressed concern of the last hour—all that worry—and there she'd been, skittering round the countryside, getting herself into danger, getting herself out of it, breaking all the laws of probability, blowing bubbles down the petrol tank, roping her man and bringing him in—and all she could say was, 'How very fortunate, Superintendent. I was so hoping we'd meet.' So hoping … So help him. Delphick held the passenger door of the police car open. He looked at the battered hat, the dishevelled little figure, mastering in his relief a strong desire to put her over his knee and smack her.

# Chapter 8

During the week that followed Miss Seeton's abduction adventure, Superintendent Delphick and Sergeant Ranger remained in Plummergen. The actual grind of collecting information, much of it useless and the remainder to be sifted and collated in the hope that it might one day be of value in the building of a case, was a slow, laborious process unimagined by the majority of the Press and public, alike impatient for finality.

On Mrs. Venning, the information so far gathered seemed innocuous except for one significant gap. She had been married at twenty-three to a rising executive in an engineering firm. The young couple, comfortably off and with an assured future, had lived a social life to the limit of their income, so that when the husband was killed in a motor accident he left his widow and two-year-old daughter with an expensive flat and no visible means of support. In neither case were the parents wealthy and, so far as could be checked, no financial help had been given to his widow. After a suitable interval, Mrs. Venning had resumed her social life, dressed well and had engaged her old nurse, a Mrs. Fratters, to help look after the child and run the flat. Sonia Venning had paid her bills, had not been in debt, but her means of support for the next three years remained a mystery. Then she had set down in book form the stories she used to invent as bed-time entertainment for her little girl. A publisher had been interested and the book had proved a success. After the publication of her second book she had sold the lease of her flat and moved to Plummergen. From then on all was plain sailing. Highly strung, gay and gregarious, she was conspicuous in all local affairs until about a year ago when she stopped all her social activities and became in effect a recluse. Her books continued to appear at regular intervals but that was all now that was known of her. Her abrupt and mysterious retirement from the life of the community had provoked, still evoked, much speculation. The police too speculated. It could be no more than the evident trouble with her daughter, but it was tempting to take the two unaccountable chapters in her life and to deliberate possible cause and effect. There appeared to have been no man other than her husband; although it would have been an obvious and easy solution to account for her solvency in the early days of her widowhood, no trace of such a man could be found. Again a love affair would have been a simple answer to her recent seclusion but in all the talk about her there was no hint of this and it was difficult to believe that the village gossips would not have seized upon the idea had there been any grounds. Indeed, with impulsive generosity, they would have provided her with not one man but a score.

In the case of Mr. Trefold Morton research was hampered by the need for delicacy. As a solicitor he could, and no doubt would, make things awkward if he got wind of their investigation. There was nothing against him. The police had no excuse for curiosity. Report made him more prominent than popular or, as one fellow councillor put it in the course of conversation, "A gas bag with influence." There was nothing tangible but the superintendent decided that there was a 'feeling'. Mr. Trefold Morton felt wrong. He was obviously well-to-do. It could, though at this stage there could be no means of proving it, that he was better-to-do than might have been expected. The only facts which emerged and which Delphick filed as of possible interest were that in four cases clients whose affairs were completely in their solicitor's hands had come to unfortunate ends: or more accurately, in three cases; in the fourth, though the present was unfortunate, the end was still to come.

A Mrs. Cummingdale, an elderly widow presumed to be rich, had died in a fire, supposedly caused by smoking in bed. Her nephew from Scotland had been loud in his surprise when she cut up for a little over six hundred pounds. The superintendent learned from people living around that she had been behaving oddly for some time before she died.

Ernest Foremason, a bachelor in his fifties, had driven his car into a wall: the wall survived. The police opinion was "Drunk in charge". Mr. Foremason had died intestate and having no relations his estate of a few hundred pounds and a mortgage on his house had gone to the Crown. Mr. Foremason, too had been thought to be wealthy.

A Miss Worlingham, a maiden lady of sixty-three, had committed suicide. She had left a will written in her own handwriting on the morning of the day that she had died, witnessed by the milk roundsman and her daily help. The document was valueless, however, as her personalty failed to cover her debts. This caused no surprise, though she had been thought to be moneyed, since during the last years of her life her behaviour had been noted as strange.

Miss Hant, another maiden lady of uncertain years, was in a private nursing-home being treated for drug addiction and was regarded as incurable. No one visited her there except her solicitor. So far as was known she was without relatives or friends. She appeared to have had money though it was now rumored that Mr. Trefold Morton was helping with her expenses out of kindness.

Odd behaviour, drunken behaviour, strange behaviour and Miss Hant's behaviour with her craving for heroin could not be counted as normal. All lonely people without close kin to question the aftermath of their death. All presumed to be rich yet all shown in the event to be poor. All except Miss Hant and even there the hint of poverty was in the offing. Coincidences worth bearing in mind? the superintendent thought so, but on the other hand, how many solicitors could not show a like percentage of unfortunate clients in the course of thirty years' practice. There was no way that he could see for the police to carry the inquiries further. It would be useless to interview Miss Hant in the nursing-home for although rational enough at times, according to her doctor, like all drug addicts she would give no helpful information to the police and he would have succeeded in advising Mr. Trefold Morton of his interest. It would be a pity to make no effort to see her while she was still alive, her doctor did not give her a long expectation, for once she was dead there would be nothing the police could do without more to go on than they had. In fact, as the superintendent admitted, they had nothing. The germ of an idea to achieve this object had occurred to him but he was still unsure whether to put the idea before his superiors, or to risk acting on his own initiative.

From the viewpoint of the police, the investigation into Miss Seeton's abduction which with the facts undisputed and the culprit in jail should have been simple, was proving to be the most difficult. They had so far failed to obtain further information of any kind and the case was verging on the ridiculous. The preliminary inquiry before the magistrate on the morning following the arrest had alerted the newspapers and reporters had flocked to the district. Birds of Press had hovered round the chief actors in the drama, pecking at stories before settling in rows with a flutter of notebooks on the Press Benches in the magistrate's court at Ashford four days later.

The case was a blessing. Apart from cheesecake, it had all the ingredients to please a newsman: a colourful heroine, a gallant rescuer who had been wounded in the fray and a mysterious villain.

The case was a curse. Apart from cheesecake, it had every ingredient to displease a policeman: a colourful heroine, a gallant rescuer who had beaten the police to it by a car's length, and a mysterious villain. This last was the greatest snag. Miss Seeton and her burly friend had handed over their prisoner to the law neatly tied, but unlabelled. The label was still missing. The prisoner refused to speak—at all. His fingerprints were not on file which suggested the amateur. He had nothing on him which gave a clue to his identity which argued the professional. The van he had used, an old Buick car converted and with the back of the body too large for the chassis, turned out to have been stolen overnight in Brettenden, the owner remaining unaware of the theft until it was returned to him. Attempts to establish his identity by publishing his photograph produced the usual spate of replies, all useless. Identification parades were held for members of The Singing Swan, for Nigel Colveden and for Angela Venning. The seven suspect members of the club and Angela were over-loudly positive that they had never set eyes on him. This evidence, though it might convince the police to the contrary, with the over-loudness muffled by defence counsel, would have the opposite effect on the Court. Of other members of the club who had been present on the night of the hen-house raid, one was certain and two were fairly sure that the prisoner had been one of a group at a corner table. Two more were definite that he had not been present. The evidence cancelled out. Nigel thought that he was one of the two strangers in the car park but the light had not been good and he could not decide without hearing the voice. Evidence mute and inconclusive.

The police considered asking for more time but came to the conclusion that if the prisoner succeeded in maintaining his silence, the longer the case was delayed the more farcical it was likely to become. In any event, the gravity of the charges, abduction and unlawful wounding presupposed that the case would be sent to the Assizes at Maidstone and this would automatically gain them time before the trial proper.

The youth had been granted legal aid and his counsel, not averse to publicity, entered the fray with enthusiasm. Having first pleaded that there was no case to answer since his client was more the victim than the aggressor, thenceforward, unhampered by any instructions from his client, he was free to let an unfettered imagination roam and it became clear at the Ashford court what line the defence would take.

The police had kept the prisoner under observation in hospital and the doctor's written report was that he could find nothing physical or organic amiss nor any overt signs of mental instability. His verbal report was more lucid: "He's boxing clever!" A doctor called by the defence agreed with the physical and organic soundness but theorised that it was impossible to stipulate what effects shock and bound incarceration in the back of a moving vehicle might have on a highly strung mind; it could well lead to temporary amnesia and loss of speech. The prosecution doctor, recalled, had to concede the point but said he could see no ground for the supposition of a highly strung mind. The defence doctor, recalled, contended that the grounds for such a supposition were the evident results. Thus the medical evidence ended in a draw with a replay booked for the Maidstone Assizes.

On the question of abduction the defence seized upon Miss Seeton's assumption of "a prank in revenge for the egg stealing" to minimise the charge and with regard to the unlawful wounding the burly van driver played into their hands by saying that "Young Ginger acted like a nut case".

The way things were going, Superintendent Delphick reflected, this wretched little hoodlum was likely to be let loose on probation as a first offender with the sympathy of the Court for his sufferings. The van driver would be fortunate if he were not charged with assault and Miss Seeton could count herself lucky if she escaped with a fine for wantonly immobilising the defendant's vehicle.

The superintendent, determined that Mr. Trefold Morton should not escape through lack of assay, resolved on an attempt to put his plan for interviewing Miss Hant into effect.

# Chapter 9

"Any luck?" asked Delphick.

"I'm afraid not, Superintendent. I did what you asked me to do. I went and saw that poor Miss Hant. Naturally I know it's all very tragic and one should feel sorry for persons like that and, of course, I do, in a way, but there are so many people in trouble through no fault of their own and I know it's very unfeeling of me, but I do find it difficult to sympathise completely with someone who's gone out of their way to bring trouble upon themselves. I did as you suggested and tried to show an interest and asked what made her start on drugs in the first place, but her replies were very rambling and frankly I doubt if they were strictly true."

"I doubt it, too. Drug addicts and alcoholics have this in common; the truth is not in them."

"I felt that she resented my intrusion and I must say I really couldn't blame her. So I fear, after all, I wasn't of any assistance to you."

"No?" An eyebrow quirked. "It was your impression of Miss Hant rather than her version of herself that I was interested in."

"My impression?" Miss Seeton looked bewildered. "But I don't think I—well, I don't think I have one."

Delphick smiled. "Not even a sketch?" He looked from her to her writing-desk: the flap was not quite shut and pieces of paper were protruding.

She followed his gaze. "That—oh, but that's quite different. I mean it has nothing to do with Miss Hant. At least not directly."

"Direct or not," argued Delphick, "the mere fact that it's something that you felt so soon after seeing Miss Hant is enough to make it interesting."

She yielded. "But of course you can look if you really want to. But really it has nothing to do with Miss Hant. It's—it's rather unkind, in fact, and perhaps—well, a trifle vulgar."

On the paper capered an obese and elderly gentleman with a European face, clad only in his dark skin, a grass skirt and a gloating expression. In his left hand he brandished a native spear; in his right hand he clutched aloft four shrunken heads. Or was it five? Four had features roughly pencilled in; the fifth was blank like an egg.

Miss Seeton was embarrassed. "I—I hadn't meant anyone to see it. And I'd no reason to ... After all, Mr. Trefold Morton's been most kind and considerate. Of course he does boom rather."

Delphick replaced the drawing, shut the desk and smiled. "Was it seeing Miss Hant that put Mr. Trefold Morton into your head?"

"Oh no," explained Miss Seeton, "he was going into the nursing-home as I was coming out. I met him in the hall."

"Damn," said Delphick.

… "But I tell you this could prove very serious for me. Very serious indeed. You don't appear to appreciate the gravity of the situation. The extreme gravity. This woman—this wretched woman—appears to be hand-in-glove with the police. Maybe working for them. Employed by them. She may be a professional spy. Something must be done about her. And done at once… . But I tell you it is urgent. The woman must have been following me about. Getting in front of me even. This morning, when I went to see Miss Hant, she was there. At the nursing-home. Just leaving. She'd been to see Miss Hant herself. Now what reason could she have for doing that? What possible reason? Dr. Knight had some trumped-up story that he'd thought it'd be a good idea for Miss Hant to have outside visitors. I don't believe a word of it. Not a word. That woman had put him up to it. Or else the police must have been behind the whole thing… . But I tell you it does matter. Of course it matters. And it's not just my concern. It's your concern as well. Don't you understand, I gave this wretched Seeton woman some pills… . No, I don't know whether she took any. I don't know what she's done with them. But if the police get hold of them … Well, it wasn't my fault. She seemed a good proposition. A perfectly sound proposition. At the time. It seemed ideal. Not rich, of course. Not really rich. But quite a nice little property. And worth picking up. Well worth it. And when she actually complained of having a headache … Yes, of course I realise it may have been a trap. I realise it now. But I couldn't have known it. I couldn't possibly have known that then. Can't you arrange something? Make some arrangements to deal with her? And deal with her effectively? … Very well, then. I'll wait here for a call."

Mr. Trefold Morton replaced the receiver, took a crisp, clean handkerchief from his breast pocket and mopped his brow.

Two hours later the telephone bell rang. He grabbed the instrument.

"Trefold Morton here."

The telephone spoke.

Mr. Trefold Morton interrupted. "Instructions? My instructions? But I mustn't be involved in any way. That would be fatal. Quite fatal. Surely you realise that someone in my position—my position in the community ..."

The telephone commented briefly on Mr. Trefold Morton's position.

"But if I 'set her up for it' as you call it, don't you realise what that could mean? Great heavens, it would mean that I would become a party to it. An accessory. I couldn't risk that. It could mean disaster for me. Disaster."

The telephone was terse.

"But—but it's in your interest, too. After all you've had the money. You insisted on a percentage. And a very good percentage of the three estates. Considering that the idea, all the work, and the risk was mine. Entirely mine. And there will be Miss Hant's to come as well. But if anything were sus-pected... . If any suspicion were to fall on me ... Oh, great heavens!"—Mr. Trefold Morton's voice was shaking—"What am I to do?"

The telephone told him.

"Very well. I suppose I shall have to. But I can't ask her to dinner. It would be ridiculous. Quite ridiculous. At such short notice. I hardly know the woman. And in any case,

137

I have a prior engagement. I'll think of something. Some papers that have to be signed. Some urgent signature. I'll drop her off at the crossroads at Plummergen Common, as you say, but anything that happens after that is nothing to do with me. Nothing at all. I want to know nothing about it. Nothing. Is that quite clear?"

The telephone agreed.

Mr. Trefold Morton pushed it away and sank back in his chair. He mopped his face again, then stuffed the handkerchief back into his breast-pocket where it hung, a limp symbol of its owner, crumpled, soiled and wet.

"It is very good of you to have taken such a forbearing attitude at my having interrupted your evening in this manner. Very good of you. It was remiss of me to have overlooked the need for your signature on that particular document. Most remiss. A little hold up of that kind, as you doubtless know, could delay the whole of probate. Or, maybe, you yourself are but a probationer in these matters." Miss Seeton winced in anticipation of the inevitable laugh. It came, but the boom was a little hollow. "However," Mr. Trefold Morton continued, "all's well that ends ..."—he faltered, recovered—"that is to say, that we should now catch the first post in the morning. Now you're sure—quite sure—that you don't mind walking home from the crossroads, if I drop you off there?"

"Not at all," murmured Miss Seeton.

"It is unfortunate that the friends with whom I should have been dining and whom I shall now have to join for coffee should live in exactly the opposite direction. Most unfortunate. But naturally I will take you right to your door, if you insist. Naturally. However late it makes me. Or, if absolutely necessary, I could telephone my friends and say that I won't be able to get there."

"Please," protested Miss Seeton, "I wouldn't hear of it. You say it's no distance to walk—less than a mile. And, in any case, I have a torch with me. It's very kind of you to have brought me so far."

"The least I could do. The very least. Besides, by using this route to the village, as far as this is on my way. It's only here that our paths diverge."

He slowed as he approached the Plummergen-Ashford road, pulled in to the side and stopped the car. Miss Seeton got out. Mr. Trefold Morton called through the window:

"Now, you know your direction? This part is called Plummergen Common. You turn to the right and the road leads straight down into the village. And you're sure you'll be all right? Quite sure? Because if so, I'll be on my way. I feel dreadful—leaving you here like this. Quite dreadful. But needs must when the—er ... Yes, indeed. Needs must."

Without giving her time to reply, the car jolted forward, clashed into second gear, turned left and sped down the road.

How that man talked. Really, she was positively tired from listening to him. Of course it was very thoughtful of him to have sent a car to fetch her to Brettenden. But, to be honest, had she realised, when he offered to give her a lift back, that he meant to drop her off here, she would have asked the driver to wait and take her home. Oh! Miss Seeton jumped as a noise like a shot sounded from a nearby field. Bird scarers? When it was dark? Ah, yes, she remembered now Stan had said something about farmers using them at

139

night to frighten rabbits and things. Surely it would have saved time if Mr. Trefold Morton had brought the papers for her to sign over to Plummergen in the first place and then gone on to his friends from there? However, she hadn't liked to suggest it on the telephone, when he'd told her that a car would be calling for her and was already on its way. No doubt it was just habit to attend to all business matters in his office. But he'd literally never stopped talking from the moment she'd arrived there. It was ridiculous, of course, but one might almost have said that he was nervous. Surely he couldn't have supposed that she might view a call to his office after hours, in the light of an assignation. Miss Seeton smiled at the thought, took her torch from her handbag and switched it on.

Now, did one walk on the right side of the road, or on the left? Cars drove on their—left, didn't they? And pedestrians? There was some rule about it. Either you did the same as cars—or exactly the opposite. Going down into a tube station there was a notice telling you to keep to the ... She tried to visualise such a notice. Ah, yes. KEEP TO THE RIGHT. So probably the same applied. She shone her torch across the road. Well, that settled it. A hedge and a ditch on that side. One might easily miss one's footing and stumble into the ditch if a car came by. So awkward when there were no pavements—no, footpaths, she believed, was the correct term in the country. Whereas over here it was comparatively flat. Of course. This would be the Common.

The headlights of a car flared up suddenly some way in front of her. Miss Seeton stepped well off the road and turned aside to keep the dazzle from her eyes.

How effective. A lake. No—probably not big enough for that. But a very large pond. She would wait by this tree till the car had passed. Curious the falsifying effect of artificial light. The leaves of the trees and shrubs overhanging the water, even the branches, looked as though they were cut out of cardboard. Yet, even as she watched, the light changed, the third dimension was added, forms grew solid. Miss Seeton glanced behind her. A car coming from the opposite direction. Distances were extraordinarily deceptive at night. The first car appeared no nearer. Seemed not to have moved. Perhaps a couple … No, because then, surely, they would have driven off the road. And then again, they wouldn't have their lights on. The lights of the second car were brilliant now. Brilliant? They were coming straight towards her. Oh dear, oh dear, there'd be an accident. What was the driver thinking of?

She waved her umbrella to attract attention, then turned to run. Blinded, she bumped into the tree, knocking her hat off, staggered round the trunk and blundered forward. There was a splintering crash as the car hit the tree against which she'd been standing.

There. She knew it.

Horrified, she turned to go to their assistance, trod on nothing, lost her balance and fell backwards with a splash.

# Chapter 10

The village grape-vine in action: something observed here; something overheard there; a meeting or two, a few discussions, some telephone calls—and the picture was coming into focus.

Miss Treeves had observed Miss Seeton's departure. Going out to supper? That was unusual. And why hire a car from Pratt's in Brettenden instead of using Crabbe's from the village? She discussed this with Martha Bloomer when they met in the church to top up the water in the flower-vases for the night and replace any dead blooms.

Doris, the waitress at The George and Dragon, had overheard the conference at table as the superintendent and his sergeant were finishing their dinner. Doris had discussed with the barmaid the facts that: Miss Seeton had gone missing again; the police were ringing up all over the shop and that the young one, the big one, was bringing the car round.

The barmaid passed the facts on to Stan Bloomer as he was finishing his evening pint. Stan told Martha on his return home and Martha went straight over to Miss Seeton's cottage where she telephoned Lady Colveden on the chance that Miss Seeton might have called there on her way back.

Lady Colveden, a late starter through not living on The Street itself, soon caught up with, then passed her competitors by the adroit use of her title and her telephone. She rang old Mr. Pratt's private number, learned that Mr. Trefold Morton had hired him, that it was he himself who had fetched Miss Seeton and taken her to the solicitor's office where he had been told not to wait as Mr. Trefold Morton would give her a lift home. Undeterred by the fact that Mr. Trefold Morton's housekeeper said that he was dining out and she didn't know where, Lady Colveden demanded a list of possible names and addresses. She struck lucky at her third attempt, insisted on speaking to the solicitor himself and when informed that he had dropped Miss Seeton off at Plummergen Common, leaving her to walk home, commented on his behaviour in terms that would have raised blisters on the hide of a rhinoceros.

Sir George was out at a meeting. Nigel, once he had grasped the purport of his mother's telephone progression, jumped up and headed for the door. Lady Colveden called after him.

"If you take the M.G. without me, I'll ... I'll ..."

Threats failing her, she had to depend on tone of voice and expression. A short call to Martha to bring her up to date, she downed receiver, snatched coat and head scarf from the hall and ran out to join her son.

Martha relayed the latest information to the police so that as the Colvedens swept round into The Street, Delphick and Bob Ranger were already pulling away from The George and Dragon opposite. The two cars stormed away, Nigel fractionally in the lead.

Arms flailing, groping hands clutched, held. Miss Seeton struggled to gain a foothold—found one—and discovered that by clinging on above and by standing on tiptoe below she could keep her chin above water.

Entirely her own fault. So very careless—not to look where she was going. Of course she had been dazzled by the lights, but she should have remembered how near she was to the pond's edge. So very fortunate, too, to find something to … She looked up. Her immediate surroundings were silhouetted against the light which shone across the water in front of her. Why—it was her own umbrella, hooked on a branch above her, that she was grasping. Some of the younger mistresses might laugh at her for carrying an umbrella in all weathers, but you never really knew. And, after all, it was practical. Now—could she, by pulling on it, get herself out? She must try to see if she could help whoever had been in that car—they might be injured, perhaps badly hurt. She heard the sound of movement and peered through the twigs and leaves. Yes. There was the car; one side crumpled against the tree, the remaining headlight still on. The car door opened and a figure got out. A young man. Well, probably. The young dressed so alike these days; very sensible but a little muddling sometimes. Miss Seeton opened her mouth to call. The figure moved forward into the light, examining the ground ahead. Long fair hair glittered.

It couldn't be—it—it was. That dreadful boy who had killed that girl in London. Miss Seeton realised she was very cold. The water of course. She shut her mouth.

The dreadful boy returned to the car, leaned in, then backed out, dragging another figure. A girl. He hefted the body, swung it above his head and … Oh, no, he couldn't— no, please—he mustn't—oh no, how truly shocking—

… smashed the head against the door jamb.

A frantic effort to get out. To stop him. Her feet slipped, her hand slipped; she slipped under water.

"Glp!" screamed Miss Seeton.

He ran to the bank and threw the body down so that it lay on the brink with the head under water. He moved forward. Looked about, around, down. A report cracked as another cartridge from the bird scarer exploded. He sprang round, crouched, pistol in hand. Lights in the distance approaching. He straightened, hesitated, then sprinted for the road. The car which Miss Seeton had first seen stationary was approaching slowly, the passenger door open. He reached it. Jumped in. The door slammed. The car accelerated.

"It's no good, Mr. Colveden, apart from the head injury, the neck's broken. She was dead before she hit the water." Reluctantly, Nigel laid the body of Angela Venning back on the grass and stood up. "We'll know more when we get the doctor's report," Delphick went on, "and when we can examine the ground by daylight. But it looks as if she lost control, tried to jump out, crashed the tree before she could make it and hit her head on the door as she was thrown out. If you'll stay here, sergeant, till the ambulance arrives, I'd better get back on the road and try to find Miss Seeton."

"Would you take my son with you, Superintendent, I'll …" Lady Colveden took a deep breath. "I feel that I should go and break the news to Mrs. Venning."

"Would you? I should be grateful, it would be kinder, I think. We'd better get on then, Mr. Colveden. Other mobile units should be along soon but we can't afford to waste time." Delphick returned to his car. As a sleepwalker, Nigel followed him.

Lady Colveden turned for a last look at the girl's body, at the wrecked car. Looked again. Ran forward and knelt.

"Sergeant." Her voice was sharp.

Bob Ranger joined her. His torch shone on the remains of Miss Seeton's hat crushed under a front wheel. Without a word, he started circling, like an enormous hound casting for a scent. His second cast brought him to the bank.

"Hold the torch."

Lady Colveden hurried to him, took the torch, held it steady. There, from a branch above the water, as it were an arrow to mark the spot, hung an umbrella. The sergeant stripped to his undershorts, stepped to the edge. The torch beam wobbled. In his clothes he was big. Out of them he looked like a colossus. If he jumped there'd be a tidal wave. And he might land on—crush ... Lady Colveden relaxed as Bob Ranger lowered himself gently into the water. The torch aimed down, probing. The sergeant, chest deep, then deeper, knelt and vanished under water, to reappear a moment later holding a sodden bundle. He put the bundle over one shoulder and clambered out.

Tragedy immanent; the night cut by a swath of light. Danger imminent; the night a festering shadow. A primeval monster rises dripping from the swamp, his capture in his arms. A horror film in action. It was too much. Lady Colveden fought to repress incipient hysteria.

The sergeant loosened the clothes, laid the little figure face downwards on the grass in the light of the remaining headlamp, knelt astride it and turned the head. He placed his hands low down on the back and began to exert pressure.

After a moment or two, Miss Seeton yielded a quantity of pond.

Lady Colveden, reaching precariously, retrieved the umbrella, collected the sergeant's clothes, took them over to her M.G. and put them in the boot. She reversed the car and left it, engine running, facing towards Plummergen.

After this moment of normal activity, the improbable reality of the scene struck her the more. One body lay half-shadowed, the other full-lit and crouched over it the bared body of a man. Emotion outrunning her capacity, Lady Colveden bit back a giggle of fright. The Monster snarls over his prey.

The sergeant thought that he detected the first faint signs of breathing. He continued the rhythmic pressure until he was certain, then turned Miss Seeton over and began to pat her face.

Some ... where. Somehow. Some thing. Must tell the Grey Day. And the Footballer. Some ... Bob Ranger bent low to catch the murmur. "Grey Day ... Football ... must ..."

He began to pat her face again. Wearily her eyes flickered open to strain through shifting mist: focused. Black against the light, a naked man squatted over her, one hand upraised to strike; descending.

Oh, no. No, please. Miss Seeton fainted.

Grateful for practical action which helped to dispel the nightmare quality of events that was threatening to overwhelm her, Lady Colveden fetched a rug from the car and as the sergeant wrapped Miss Seeton's unconscious form:

"Dr. Knight's. That's the quickest," she told him. "We turn right before the village and it's almost opposite the lane to the Vennings'. I'll drop you there and then go on to The Meadows to tell them of the accident."

As they were starting, the ambulance arrived. She stopped. The sergeant left a message for Delphick, gave brief instructions to the men to await the superintendent's return and they were off.

Drawing up outside what had once been the old Cottage Hospital, Sergeant Ranger got out, rang the bell, went in, still carrying Miss Seeton and the door of the little nursing-home swung to behind him.

Lady Colveden's M.G. pulled away and took the turning opposite, to The Meadows. She drove slowly down the lane, dreading the coming interview. It proved to be worse that she had feared. Sonia Venning flatly refused to believe her; refused to discuss Angela; refused to go upstairs and check that the girl was, as she maintained, in her room and stated that the car was in the garage which was locked, producing the key to the padlock from her bag as proof. Helpless in the face of this rejection, Lady Colveden began to feel desperate. Mrs. Venning turned abusive, shouting that the village, the police, that everybody was against them, persecuting them. That Angela had been a little thoughtless and wild, but that she was completely able to deal with her. And had. Disturbed by the noise, Mrs. Fratters came from the kitchen to see what was the matter. Lady Colveden appealed to her.

Mrs. Fratters beamed. "Miss Angie? Oh no, m'lady. She's upstairs in her bed, she's not been well these last few days, you see. She had her supper in bed, I took it up to her myself."

But the police would come, questioning. And find them unprepared. Lady Colveden struggled to free them, to free herself, from this fantasy, this engulfing miasma of disbelief.

"She's not in bed. She's dead, I tell you, dead. Oh, God, how can I make you understand? She's dead. She's by the pond on the Common, lying there, dead. Her car hit a tree. She nearly killed Miss Seeton. She's ..." Catching the note of hysteria in her voice, she set her teeth hard on her lower lip.

Mrs. Fratters had left the room. The two women remained frozen. A sobbing wail and the housekeeper was back.

"It's true, ma'am. She's gone. The window's open. And there's a ladder. She's gone. Oh, ma'am, m'lady, what are we to do?"

"Liar!" shrieked Mrs. Venning. "You're all lying." She swung round, plunged blindly out.

Lady Colveden grabbed the telephone and dialled. "Dr. Knight? Meg Colveden, at Mrs. Venning's. Can you come over at once? She needs help."

Sonia Venning stood in the doorway, wild-eyed, in her hand a padlock, hasp and staple, splinters of wood still clinging to it. "You were lying. An accident, you said. What accident put a ladder to her window?" Her voice rose. "What accident did this?" She shook the padlock. "Angela never forced that, she hasn't the strength. Who did it? Who phoned her? Answer me. Who telephoned this evening? Who was with her?"

"Why nobody," stammered Lady Colveden. But something glimmered in her mind "She—she was alone."

"She wasn't," snarled the other. "The Seeton woman was there. You said so. Who else? Go on, tell me, who else? Who did it?"

"There was nobody." Again the glimmer. Yet surely, there must ...

"There was. There was." The voice cracked higher. "There must have been. You killed her. And you call it an 'accident'."

Dr. Knight hurried into the room. One glance and he forced the distraught mother to a chair, stood across it, caught her arm and imprisoned it against his side.

"She drugged by accident," the frantic voice babbled on, "that accident was mine, my fault, the fault was mine. She died by accident. Who's accident was that? Not mine. Oh God, not mine."

"In my bag, on top, the hypodermic in a tin box, cotton swabs and the bottle of spirit next to it, quickly, please." The doctor's calm voice was a moment of sanity. Lady Colveden fumbled, found them, held them ready. The doctor peeled back the sleeve, swabbed, filled the cylinder, inserted the needle and pushed the plunger home.

"Tell me," the voice was screaming, "tell me, go on, tell me, murderer, whose accident was that?" The raving faded to a murmur and stopped.

Except for Mrs. Fratters's helpless sobbing, silence across the room.

A nursing-home? There must be some mistake. Bob gaped at the rather plain little girl in pigtails who had paused halfway down the staircase to stare back at him in a moment of equal bewilderment. She pulled her dressing-gown tighter—not such a little girl as he'd supposed.

Not another accident? What a day. Well, at least they weren't dripping blood all over the place—like that poor wretched ploughman this morning who'd cut half his finger off—Good Lord—it looked as if he'd got that Miss Seeton who'd called on the Hant female. Not dead. Or he wouldn't have brought her here. And if there was no blood, they were certainly dripping. She ran back up the stairs, calling over her shoulder:

"Up here. First door on the right."

His clothes and Miss Seeton's umbrella under one arm, Miss Seeton herself cradled in the other, Bob went up after her. Entering the first door on his right he found that an electric fire had been switched on, the bars beginning to redden and a large bath towel laid in front of it. The plain girl with the pigtails was taking a nightdress and some small towels from a chest of drawers. On a table by the bed glowed the orange light of an adjustable electric top blanket. Bob dropped his clothes and the umbrella near the door and laid Miss Seeton on the carpet beside the towel. Working together with the silent efficiency of a practiced team, they stripped her, dried her and slipped her into the nightdress.

In the doorway, Dr. Knight stood watching them. "I would of course be the last to interfere if this is a purely private affair. However, should you need the services of a doctor at any time, don't hesitate to call on me."

The plain girl looked up with a smile. "Ah, there you are, Dad. Good. I was just coming for you as soon as we'd got her into bed. I think she's all right. The breathing's not bad and the pulse is quite strong, though a little fast."

"Right. Anne. I'll have a look at her. To save time, you might fetch my bag. Anything I want will be there. I'm sure that your probationer is quite strong enough, from the looks of him, to put the lady to bed on his own. I'll be here to keep an eye on the proprieties and to see that he knows which end the head goes and technical points of that kind."

Bob picked Miss Seeton up and laid her on the bed as Anne went out and the doctor leaned forward, pulled back an eyelid to examine the pupil, then felt the pulse. Anne came back with his bag. He took his stethoscope, listened to Miss Seeton's chest, then straightened.

"Shall we turn her for you, Dad?"

"No-o. I don't think that's necessary. At a guess, I should say immersion followed by shock." He took a hypodermic syringe from a box in his bag while Anne produced cotton wool and a bottle of spirit from a drawer in the bedside table and swabbed Miss Seeton's upper arm. "A sedative," the doctor went on as he injected, "that's the best thing. She'll sleep right through and that, with warmth, should take care of the shock. As to the immersion, I doubt there'll be any complications, but at her age you can never be sure. We shall know tomorrow. Since it's that Miss Seeton that everybody's so interested in, I think, Anne, you should ring The George and Dragon and tell that superintendent fellow that we've got his lady friend here. You had better, perhaps, mention that it would appear that she had been bathing, unseasonably and unsuitably clad. And that he can see her tomorrow morning, but not before."

"Right, Dad." Anne crossed to a corner cupboard, collected a kidney-shaped white enamel bowl, took a hypodermic from it, dropped the used one in its place, clipped the fresh one into her father's case and slipped it into his bag. Carrying the bowl, she turned to the door as the telephone rang.

"Blast!" said Dr. Knight.

"Shall I take it, Dad?"

"No, my dear. I'd better go and learn the worst. It's bound to be somebody giving birth to a clowder of kittens. It always is. And they always do—after hours. And the later, the bigger the litter," he called back as he sped down the stairs.

152

Anne became conscious of Bob staring at her and embarrassment made her brisk. "I was on the point of having a bath when you arrived. You'd better take it over, it'll only need some more hot water. If you like to bring your clothes, I'll show you where the bathroom is." She picked up Miss Seeton's sodden garments, balancing the enamel bowl on top.

It dawned on Bob, in horrid revelation, that he was not dressed—not dressed at all—for a social occasion. As his face flamed and he bent to retrieve his clothes, he had a moment's fleeting thankfulness that he didn't wear those rather tight triangular briefs that were so fashionable. At least his own loose undershorts were decent. He glanced down. But not, he realised, when wet. His colour mounting to a rich shade of petunia, he dropped his clothes, grabbed the towel from the floor and pulled it round his waist. He hung Miss Seeton's umbrella on the door and recovered his clothes. Anne watched him with an expression of grave interest, but Bob caught the glint of laughter in her eyes.

"Of course," she remarked, "I don't know if you can talk. But so long as you can understand ..." Bob sweated and cleared his throat, preparing to apologise—to explain—to say ... what on earth could he say? "Don't try," Anne reassured him kindly. "There's no need to speak. It's just nice to know that you probably could. If you wanted to. Come along."

She closed the door behind them and set off down the passage, Bob following: a leviathan in tow to a tiny tug.

With Bob settled in the bathroom, she disposed of Miss Seeton's clothes and the basin, then repaired to her bedroom where she rang The George and Dragon, left a message, sat down at her dressing-table and looked at her reflection.

Damn. Damn. Damn.

And again, damn.

Her face was hopeless, of course, but her hair was pretty and her figure good. It would be just her luck, concluded Anne as she studied her reflection with distaste, that the former should be screwed up in pigtails for a bath, while the latter was hidden under pyjamas and a serviceable but shapeless dressing-gown. She pulled the offending ribands out of her hair, brushed it, dressed quickly, choosing something red that clung, then ran downstairs.

A drink. And a snack. Perhaps coffee? He must have something after plunging about in the canal, or the pond, or wherever—or he'd catch a cold. Her mother had gone with friends to the cinema in Brettenden and wouldn't be back yet, so she was free to forage. She noted her father's message on the telephone-pad by the hall extension. "Gone Vennings," wondered briefly what was up, dismissed it and continued on her way to the kitchen. Once there, she paused. What would a snack be for someone of that size? A whole ham, a loaf of bread and suet pudding to follow? She began to put things on the trolley. Slices of ham, mustard, pickles, bread, butter, cheese and a jam-tart That should do. She pushed the trolley into the sitting-room, plugged in the percolator, put out the drinks and, hearing Bob on the stairs, went into the hall. The front door opened and her father came in followed by the superintendent.

Just her luck.

# Chapter 11

Many of the villagers had a busy and satisfying evening. Facts were plentiful, fancies abounded and rumours flew.

Miss Seeton was missing, gone off in a car—fact. The sound of shots had been heard—fact. Nigel Colveden, with his mother, had raced down The Street, hotly pursued by the police—fact. The Vennings' car was smashed against a tree by the pond on The Common—fact. An ambulance had driven away from the scene of the crash—fact. Lady Colveden had driven in the opposite direction accompanied by a man without a stitch on—fact. Nigel Colveden was in a police car with the superintendent from London—fact. Two police cars were drawn up by the pond and the officers refused to allow anybody near—fact.

Nigel Colveden was under arrest—not exactly a fact, but what other explanation could there be? Angela Venning was drunk and had driven off the road with several of her friends from the club; they were all in the ambulance—well, if not a fact, it was only too likely, wasn't it? There were things by the pond too horrible to be seen—must be a fact, surely. There'd been a gun battle on the Common—an audible fact.

Miss Seeton had fled—evidently a fact. Lady Colveden was old enough to know better—an undisputed fact.

Miss Seeton had fled; possibly to London; probably abroad. Miss Seeton had caused the accident, attacked Angela Venning and her friends and, always ready with that revolver of hers, had shot three and wounded one; the bodies had been taken away in the ambulance. The bodies were laid out in a row by the edge of the pond and guarded by police; the ambulance had rushed a wounded man to the Ashford Hospital for a blood transfusion. There had been a moonlight bathing party which the police had raided; Lady Colveden had got away with Nigel, but without his clothes. Lady Colveden had absconded with one of the men. Angela Venning and one, two, three of her friends had been drowned and taken away by ambulance. Angela Venning had crashed her car trying to escape and she and two, three, four of her friends had been rushed to the Ashford hospital, by ambulance, in a critical condition. Miss Seeton had made a getaway driving the ambulance. Miss Seeton had been found drugged in the pond and had been taken away by ambulance. Miss Seeton was still in the pond, refusing to come out and the police were on the bank trying to persuade her. Nigel Colveden had been arrested: for fighting Miss Seeton; for fighting Angela and her friends; for fighting the police; for indecent exposure.

It was deplorable. It was tragic. It was shocking.

Admittedly all these allegations were but kite-flying. However, they were worth the enjoyment spent on them, since there was the knowledge, born of experience, that with a little tailoring here and a touch of embroidery there a fair proportion of them would be deemed to have achieved factual status by the morning.

Most of the police had a busy, if not wholly satisfying, night. Delphick blamed himself. He should have cottoned on to the fake accident. He should not have allowed the body to be moved, nor let people trample the ground, until the police surgeon and the murder squad had arrived. He should have found Miss Seeton earlier. He should have been able with luck to get a statement from her.

"She said nothing, Bob? Nothing at all?"

"No, sir. Not really. She was trying to say something. I think it was about her school. Exams, perhaps. It sounded like Grade A. Then Ball—it was more like Football, really, but it couldn't have been that. Then Must—or Just. Then her eyes opened and she suddenly looked scared silly and passed out cold."

He should not have allowed the killer time to get clear before a call could be put out. He should have broken the news to Mrs. Venning himself. He should not have allowed Dr. Knight to put the only two possible witnesses incommunicado until morning. Above all, he should have managed somehow to have been in three places at once.

"Stop beefing, Oracle, about all the might-have-beens and the never-looked-like-its. Start counting your blessings for a change." Chief Detective Inspector Brinton of the Ashford Criminal Investigation Department picked up a small pile of papers and began to deal them face upward on to his desk, as if preparing for a game of solitaire. "Now, the Venning girl first." He took the top of three overlapping sheets. "A preliminary canter from our medic. 'Time of death ...' Well, we know that near enough. 'Cause of death. Fracture of left temporal area and a fracture-dislocation of the left cervical vertebrae ...'—all that the Latin for she died of a hole in

157

the head, or a broken neck—or both. 'There are also signs of contusions around both ankles …'—chummy probably gripped her by 'em. 'Marks on both thighs give a strong suggestion of the use of a hypodermic needle: may well have been a drug addict …'—all this, of course, is subject to the usual ifs and buts and why can't we wait for a proper post mortem—except that he'd call it autopsy because it's more difficult to pronounce—when he'd tell all." The chief inspector considered the next paper. "Ah, yes, our Scientific Branch. Clever lot. Write Greek. Latents on steering-wheel and door—What's the poor twit think he's talking about? If it's latent it's damn well invisible. He probably thinks Latent is the Chinese for fingerprint. I'm all for science, but save me the jargon. I'd be in favour of a computer if I wasn't afraid it'd give me the answers in Arabic. What it boils down to is: the girl's dabs on the car, padlock and garage door are mostly overlaid by smudges—so chummy wore gloves and was probably driving." He pushed the paper aside and looked at the next. "Ah, yes. The car. Nothing wrong with it. No brake failure or what-have-you. No skid marks on road. So it was deliberately driven off the road and into the tree. But not very hard. Just enough to mess up the front a bit. Chummy wanted it to look like an accident, but was careful not to hurt himself. Oh, and—yes—a woman's hat, crushed under the near front wheel.

Sergeant Ranger sat up. "That was Miss Seeton's."

"Was it? Didn't you say, Oracle, that she was fit to be tied because they mucked up her titfer when they bagged her in the sack?"

Delphick grinned. "Yes. I think it was what annoyed her most."

"On recent form she'd do better with a crash helmet." He glanced at the next set of papers. "Trefold Morton. Looks like you've hooked a tidy fish there. We picked him up for you at his friend's house and bunged him over to Brettenden to cool off. The inspector wanted to bring him here, but I said no, I thought he'd do better in his home town. Very impressed the inspector was and said, 'Ah, yes. Bringing psychological pressure to bear', which is French for using your nut."

"How's he coming along, Chris?" asked Delphick.

"Morton? Oh, quite nicely, I think. Very blustery to start with, but the wind's dying down a bit now." He pushed the top paper to one side. "I had a chat with Brettenden on the phone half an hour ago and they think he's beginning to come apart at the seams. Anyway they'll sit with him and hold his hand till you want him. By which time he should be ready to sob it all out on your shoulder. Particularly if you find anything in his office or in his house." Brinton scanned the next note. "That's all laid on. I rang Sir George Colveden. He'll have the search warrants ready and you can pick them up on your way back. He sounded delighted. At a meeting and missed all the fun earlier on, I gather."

"Yes," agreed Delphick, "but luckily he was back by the time I took young Colveden home. I felt sorry for that boy. He's a trier. Your first corpse is no fun; especially when you're young and it was someone you knew. I made him drive me. Not strictly according to regulations perhaps, but it helped to keep his mind on the road, instead of other things. His father should be able to sort him out. They're a close family."

"One more thing about Morton." The chief inspector prodded another piece of paper. "Remember, Oracle, you rang me from the Yard about The Singing Swan?"

"I did. On a tip-off from Miss Seeton."

"It would be. That woman gets her umbrella into everything. Well, I told you that we'd raided once or twice, but were pretty sure that they'd caught the whisper. We've found where the leak was. Or rather it's up and found us. When Morton was taken into the station at Brettenden, one of the local flat-feet said, well, good gracious him. If it weren't Councillor Trefold Morton—him that was always on about what a disgrace The Singing Swan was. It came out that every time we were going to raid, this idiot in uniform proudly told Morton, to show how on the ball we were and because he didn't like criticism of the force. Well, he's now learning all about criticism of the force at first hand." Brinton leaned back in his chair with a sigh. "Well, that's the lot, I think. I suppose you two want to get weaving if you're ever to get to bed tonight, though I wouldn't give much for your chances. By the way, Sergeant"—he eyed Bob severely—"what's this note from the ambulance men, that you were gambolling about Plummergen Common in female company and driving round the countryside all starkers?"

Bob's face flamed. "I was all wet, sir," he explained.

"I see." The chief inspector nodded. "Well, I won't argue with you, you should know and they say self-knowledge is the first step to wisdom."

"Lay off him, Chris," laughed Delphick. "If it hadn't been for Bob and his skin-diving act, we should have lost Miss Seeton."

"Quite. Well, I haven't met the lady myself, but before she came we just had nice quiet larcenies, dopings, muggings and the like. But since her arrival, it's been shootings, abductions and now murders—the lot. I suppose you wouldn't like to take her back to London with you and give us all a rest?"

"I believe she's considering settling down in Plummergen, Chris," Delphick told him cheerfully.

"She is, is she? Well, at the rate she's going we'd do better to call in the army and settle for martial law. Break Morton down if you can, Oracle. At the moment he's only assisting us. But if we're to hold him we'll have to work out what charges. I'll stay put till you're through with him. Even it it means dossing down here for the night."

Delphick and Bob Ranger drove from Ashford to Plummergen, called at Rytham Hall for the search warrants, then dropped in at Sweetbriars.

The superintendent was becoming almost superstitious with regard to Miss Seeton's sketches, details from which appeared increasingly relevant. He wished to study them again for any points that he might have missed before using the search warrants and particularly before seeing Mr. Trefold Morton.

They found a portfolio in the bottom drawer of the writing-desk and, on untying the tapes, amongst some sketches that fell out was one that brought an explosion of laughter from Delphick. The sergeant, in footballer's rig and with a bemuddled expression, was running, the ends of a long striped woollen scarf streaming behind him. Ahead of him, dragging him with one hand and with an umbrella in the other, her face a recognisable likeness of Miss Seeton herself, ran the Red Queen.

"Faster. Faster," chortled Delphick. "Sorry, Bob, but that's exactly how you looked at Bow Street the first night we met her."

"That does look like how she often makes me feel," Bob admitted. "But how on earth could she know I play for our police eleven?"

"What a cartoonist she'd have made," commented Delphick. He put the drawing back, took the Venning and the two Trefold Morton sketches, spread them on a table and sat down to study them. "This is almost exactly how the girl was lying," remarked the superintendent, pointing to the Niobe sketch. "We ought to have taken the warning more seriously. I did worry about it—but not enough. And then, the broken bottle. Presumably pills again."

"You mean there's a connection with this one," asked Bob, pointing to the first of the Trefold Morton drawings, "where he's holding up that phial thing of pills?"

"Maybe. It's very possible. It was a tube of pills that Trefold Morton had given her that Mrs. Venning knocked out of her hand. And Miss Seeton herself thought that was the only reason that she'd put it in the sketch—that it happened to be in her mind at the time. But, somehow ... no. I don't think so. I think it goes deeper than that. The more I look at it, the more it seems to me that this drawing should be complete in itself. An almost exact analogy. Something the mother had done, that annoyed the gods. The gods, in revenge, have killed the daughter. The mother's remorse. And the pills should fit into that story somewhere. Any connection with these"—he pushed the sketch to one side and drew the two of Trefold Morton towards him—"would only be coincidental. Now this ..." He brooded over the grass-skirted gentleman capering with the shrunken heads. "I'm fairly sure that I know what this means. Embezzlement and breach of trust. And if we're lucky we may find proof of it tonight. We'd better ..."

"Sir." Bob, who had been wandering around the room, was peering at the signature E.D.S. on a watercolour over the fireplace. The dark outline of a branch in the right foreground, a few scattered leaves still clinging, heightened the effect of distance to the grey sky where lighter and darker tones became massed and rolling clouds. Between, a sweep of moorland with heather bent before the wind. It seemed familiar.

Delphick glanced up. "Well, what is it?"

"I think it's you, sir."

Delphick got up and went over to him. "What d'you mean, you think it's me?"

"The picture, sir. I kept looking at it and thinking it was somewhere I knew. And then I suddenly realised"—Bob beamed, delighted with himself—"it's not somewhere, it's someone. Can't you see it?"

"It looks rather cold," observed Delphick.

Bob grinned. "Yes, sir. But a nice-looking picture on the whole, wouldn't you say?"

"Don't be insubordinate."

"But don't you see, sir," Bob hurried on, "it explains what Miss Seeton was trying to say. I mean, if that drawing of me reminds you of Bow Street and her first impression of me was as a footballer, then this could be her first impression of you. It was nothing to do with exams. Not Grade A. Grey day. 'Grey day ... footballer ... must ...' There was something she felt she must tell us. And that means ..."

"That her first impressions are linked with young César. Which makes it a certainty, rather than a possibility, that

163

it was Lebel with the Venning girl tonight." Delphick picked up his overcoat and shrugged himself into it. "Get cracking, we must be on our way; we've hardly started yet."

They picked up Mr. Trefold Morton's keys at the police station in Brettenden on their way to his house where they rang several times, knocked and were on the point of letting themselves in with a key when the door was opened for them by an elderly woman in dressing-gown and slippers, with a shawl round her shoulders. She had a broad face which should have been jovial, had it not been for the tiny, pursed mouth and she stood, blinking nervously at them, barring their entrance. The superintendent explained that they were police officers and apologised for the lateness of the call. She stepped back and, as soon as they were in the hall, shut the front door, then pointed to an oak bench against the wall. Delphick produced one of the search warrants, but she shook her head, pointed once more towards the bench and moved to the stairs. Nonplussed for a moment, Delphick went after her holding out the warrant. She waved it aside, drew herself up and, the little mouth pinched even tighter, jabbed her forefinger twice towards the bench with an air of command.

The sergeant was surprised to see The Oracle suddenly smile and bow.

"Very well, madam. We will wait. But we should be grateful if you'd be as quick as possible."

She gave him a brief, final nod and scuttled up the stairs.

Bob followed his superior as Delphick moved to the bench and sat down.

"What's up, sir? I don't think she's all there."

"Your powers of observation do you credit. She's not. However, I think she's repairing the omissions. We'll hope it doesn't take too long."

"But hadn't we better make a start, sir? It's getting a bit late."

"True. But I think it might save time in the long run to have a guided tour. Also there's no point in upsetting the old lady more than we need. Remember that, whatever we may think of this wretched solicitor, she probably thinks the sun, the moon and several stars shine out of him. Again, if we're lucky enough to find anything here, a witness who's prejudiced in his favour is to our advantage."

"Good evening, gentlemen."

Bob turned and his jaw dropped. Down the stairs sailed the same dressing-gown, the same shawl, the same slippers, but a woman transformed. Spectacles, with a heavy black frame, made her eyes appear large, shining and genial. The firm, wide mouth, stretched in a welcoming smile, seemed to Bob's awestruck gaze to be crammed with glistening white teeth. The whole face glittered with glass and plastic.

"I'm the housekeeper," she went on. "Can I help you? I'm so sorry to have kept you, I'm sure. The bell woke me and thinking it was him and having forgotten his key I came down quick as I could and went and quite forgot my glasses. And it wasn't a mite of good you going on about what you wanted until I'd fetched them because what you can't see you can't take in if you know what I mean. Now, what's he gone and done? There was a Lady Colven or some such name rang up earlier wanting to know where he was but as I told her I couldn't tell her not knowing. But she wouldn't take no and asked who he might be dining with so I gave her a list of possibles. But he did take his car that I do know. Has he had an accident?"

Delphick was fazed by this piece of verbiage after her determined silence at their first encounter.

"No," he assured her, "nothing like that."

"Not? But you said you were police." She beamed upon them inquiringly. "What's he been up to? Got himself into trouble?"

The superintendent chose his words with care. "There are certain matters that need an explanation. At the moment Mr. Trefold Morton is helping us with our inquiries. Have you been with him long?"

"Well 'long' depends on how you look at it, doesn't it. Now it would be—let me see …" the housekeeper considered, "yes, it would be a matter of twelve years come Christmas."

"And yet the possibility of trouble doesn't seem to surprise you?"

"Not to say surprise no. Too smooth by half I've always thought him."

"Have you had any trouble with him yourself?"

"Not to say trouble bar a couple of run-ins first off, when I came. He said the food was too expensive and I ought to be able to manage with cheaper. I told him. You can't make an omelette without breaking eggs I told him and if you want to eat the shells, sir, you're welcome if that's what you want and I'll have the eggs but lower myself I won't. He never said no more. You have to be firm or people take advantage. And then there was the wages. He wanted to keep back part of my wages and put it into something for me. I told him straight. You put my wages into my hand I told him and any further putting that needs doing I'll do myself. Too smooth by half I thought that."

The sergeant had moved unobtrusively behind the housekeeper, his notebook in his hand and Delphick decided to glean what he could while she was in the mood for reminiscence.

"Tell me," he asked, "have you noticed anything strange? Any odd goings-on?"

The housekeeper bristled. "Certainly not. Nothing of the kind. Goings-on and I'd not have stopped. Nasty he may be and not to be expected different it being his nature poor man but respectable I'm bound to give him."

Delphick pacified her. "No, that wasn't what I meant. I was thinking more of any unusual type of visitor. Or anything unusual, in fact, that you remember."

The housekeeper moved to a chair and sat down. "Well, there's one man. He comes here quite a bit, you might say he was unusual, anyway his clothes are and his hair's done in a sort of bob with a fringe. I've seen him about the town and somebody did tell me his name but it's gone, they said he runs a club or some such out Les Marys way."

"And you say he comes here quite a bit?"

"Well, you could say quite a bit—about once a week regular. Mostly latish, I've only let him in a few times myself, but sometimes when I've heard the door go late I've looked out the window and seen him leaving."

"Any others?" Delphick queried casually.

"Not to say unusual, no." She pondered a moment, then laughed. "Of course, there was the young gentleman from Scotland, but that was years back."

The superintendent's face took on a look of sympathetic interest. "Yes?"

"Well, he called, and I asked him to wait, but when I went in and gave his name, he said to say he wasn't at home, so I went back and said he wasn't in, which wasn't true of course but I couldn't say different having been told, and the young man wasn't half wild, said he'd come all the way from Scotland to bury his auntie and where was the money? I told him I couldn't say I'm sure and he stamped off saying he'd have the law on him. That made me laugh, I mean how can you have the law on a lawyer, doesn't make sense."

Delphick gave another gentle prompt. "Anyone else?"

"Else? Well, let's see now—there was that Miss ... no, her name's gone, though it was all in the papers after, she came twice. The first time he saw her and they didn't half have a row, I could hear them in the kitchen, she was shouting and screaming and she was crying when she left and he said I wasn't to let her in again if she came. But she did come, oh, a long time after, must have been above a year, it was in the morning and I said she ought to try his office but she said she'd been there and they'd said he wasn't in. She seemed in such a state I felt sorry for her, poor thing, and took her into my own room and gave her a cup of tea. She kept saying the bank must have made a mistake and she couldn't be poor, she shouldn't be poor and did I think she was poor and things like that. Well, I told her I really couldn't say, not knowing. And she said look what things had brought her to—well she did look bad and that's a fact. And she said if she wasn't poor, she kept harping on that, well anyhow if she wasn't, she'd fooled him she said and he'd find out soon enough because she'd made a new will only that morning with the milkman.

Well, that didn't make sense because milkmen don't make wills anyone knows that. Then she said never trust a solicitor, so I told her I wouldn't and was there anything I could do and she said no, there was nothing anybody could do now. And off she went. I felt quite upset. Then I read in the papers next morning how she'd gone and jumped off a roof that very afternoon after leaving here. It gave me quite a turn. I knew at the time that tea wasn't doing her any good."

"And?" Delphick still spoke quietly, afraid to break the flow.

"And?" repeated the housekeeper. "Now let's see. The only other one I can think of is a Miss Hant. Yes, now I come to think of it she wasn't so long ago, a matter of months. She turned up all wild-eyed and starey like that other Miss … funny how that name's gone and it's on the tip of my tongue too if only I could put my hand on it." She frowned.

"Miss Worlingham?" murmured Delphick.

"There of course, Worlingham, I knew I knew it if only I could call it to mind. Well, as I was saying this Miss Hant came of an afternoon, I didn't take to that one, when she must have known he wouldn't be here and was very surprised he was out or said she was but I didn't believe her, she was sly that one. She said he'd promised her some pills, well he's not a doctor I told her, but she got a bottle out of her bag and said would I pop up to his bathroom cupboard and see if there was one like it there and get it for her."

Delphick seemed almost asleep. "What kind of bottle?"

The housekeeper smiled and nodded. "Well now it's funny you should mention that. It was sort of different in a way. It started off more like a tube for tablets and then right at the bottom it opened out like a bottle. I gave her the rightabout quick, the idea that I'd go handing out his things to people at the door without directions, whatever next, and anyway there was no bottle like that in his cupboard as I should know having dusted. And he wasn't half wild when I told him, he said the woman was mad and ought to have a certificate. I hardly liked to look at the papers the next few days in case she'd done herself too, but I've heard since that she's in hospital so she's all right, I think the National Health's wonderful, don't you?"

Delphick rose hastily. "Now perhaps, if it's not keeping you up too late, you could just show us round. Have you any idea where Mr. Trefold Morton is most likely to keep any private papers?"

"Papers?" The housekeeper deliberated. "No I couldn't say, I'm sure, excepting for his office. Of course there's that safe he's got hidden behind some books in his study, you might try there I suppose." She crossed the hall and opened a door. The detectives followed her. One wall of the study had been shelved making a floor to ceiling bookcase. They exchanged glances. The conducted tour was paying off. The housekeeper took a few volumes from one of the middle shelves, disclosing a small wall safe. "There. I came on it when I had the books out for dusting but I never let on I knew not being my business, but seeing you're police with a warrant and his keys I suppose it's all right."

More than all right, Delphick reflected; blind luck. It could have taken them hours of searching, certainly more time than they had that night, to find the safe. He was intrigued, too, by the housekeeper's relation to Mr. Trefold Morton and the fact that she would not—probably, though unconsciously, could not—bring herself to mention his name, always referring to her employer as him, or he. In view of such dislike it was curious that she should have stayed with him so long. He caught himself wondering what Miss Seeton would have made of the housekeeper in one of her portraits. He selected a key from the owner's ring, opened the safe and removed the contents: a few old jewel cases; and papers. He put the cases back, handed half the papers to Bob and began to riffle through the remainder.

Entries in a small black notebook caught his attention and he put the rest to one side. The entries were under four main headings; each heading being the shortened, underlined version of a name. Under these headings followed lists of figures and dates, the earliest dating back some fifteen years, with occasional initials. The names Delphick could guess. C'dale would be Mrs. Cummingdale; the young gentleman from Scotland's auntie. F'son, Mr. Foremason who had died in a car crash. While W'ham must be Miss Worlingham. And H't could only stand for Miss Hant. A right-hand column in each entry was given over to addition and under the total was drawn a heavy black line. Delphick was struck by notes in red under the black lines: twenty-five per cent, then a figure and, after subtraction, a final total. Who, he speculated, had been milking Mr. Trefold Morton for twenty-five per cent? Miss Hant's entry was unfinished, the addition incomplete, the black line as yet undrawn. The entries were too cryptic to be resolved without a key, but his own suspicions, allied to the housckeeper's revelations filled in the picture. The figures and dates probably related to the transfer of bonds, stock and share certificates and the like, but advice from the various banks on their late client's original holdings should soon decipher the whole. He shut the book and turned to the sergeant.

"I think this is all we shall need for the moment. The rest can wait till tomorrow."

"I was wondering about these, sir." Bob offered a packet of papers, held by an elastic band.

"What are they?"

"There's no name or anything, sir, just figures. But they're dated for each week and they look like a list of outgoings and incomings. I got the idea, from what this lady told us,"—he smiled at the housekeeper—"that they might be a weekly statement of accounts from that club The Singing Swan."

Delphick took the papers, glanced at them, then, with the notebook, put them into his pocket. He returned the rest to the safe, locked it and replaced the books on the shelf. He addressed the housekeeper.

"Thank you for your patience. We shan't want anything else tonight. I'll arrange for a full search in the morning. I'm only sorry that we had to get you out of bed."

She smiled. "Oh, that's all right, it makes a change." She closed the study door. "Will he be coming back tonight?"

"No," said Delphick. "Not tonight."

Her smile broadened. "Well it just goes to show doesn't it, I told you he was smooth."

Delphick's curiosity got the better of him. "Frankly, I'm surprised you've stayed with him so long."

"Well it suited if you know what I mean," she explained. "He knows his place and I know mine and we don't interfere with each other above half. It's not as if he were married or had a family with everybody wanting things different."

"And yet I gather that you've never really liked him?"

172

"Not to say like no," she admitted amiably. "I can't abide him, never could take to him not from the first. When somebody's too smooth like he is then somebody else is going to get the rough of it I always say."

Which was as good a sum up as any of Mr. Trefold Morton and his activities, decided Delphick, as he and the sergeant returned to their car.

* * *

At the solicitor's office in the High Street they found nothing of immediate interest except for a small, unlabelled bottle of pills in a medicine cupboard on the wall of a washroom adjacent to Mr. Trefold Morton's sanctum. It was a replica of the bottle that the housekeeper had described. Held in the hand it resembled a phial, but in fact the base widened out like a miniature decanter.

"Makes it easier to stand up, I suppose," commented Bob.

"That, yes," agreed Delphick. "But more important, I should say; without being particularly noticeable, it's sufficiently different not to be mistaken for anything else."

The clock at Brettenden Police Station showed one minute to two when the superintendent and the sergeant arrived. They went straight to the office where Mr. Trefold Morton was being detained and took over the interview from the two weary officers who had run out of questions, out of ideas and had but one thought between them, sleep. Without speaking, Delphick sat down at the desk and began to read through the notes left ready for him, ignoring the solicitor's protest.

Listening, Bob decided that there was little of literary merit in Mr. Trefold Morton's repetitious phrases and contented himself with entering in his notebook: "T.M. snorting and blowing like a grampus." It took Delphick less than seven minutes from the time of their entry, to cut through the skin and reduce the whale to blubber. The superintendent had used one of those minutes before he pushed the papers to one side, stared at the solicitor, then introduced himself and the sergeant by name and rank.

Mr. Trefold Morton jumped to his feet, taking his stand on Outrage. It was an outrage, he insisted, an outrage, he repeated, in fact he repeated it several times, that he should have been kept there so long simply because he had given Miss Seeton a lift in his car. If anything had happened to her after he had dropped her—he knew nothing, of course; he had been told nothing; merely questioned like a common malefactor—but if anything had, it had nothing to do with him. Nothing at all. Nor, he ended triumphantly, if unwisely, could it be proved.

Delphick cut the ground from under him by agreeing that, on the evidence that they had so far, he was, as yet, merely an important witness in a case of murder and attempted murder. The solicitor's eyes bulged. The question of complicity would be gone into—and gone into very thoroughly—at a later stage. And that, if that had been the only reason for his detention, it would indeed have been an outrage.

"I understand," he continued, "that the manager of The Singing Swan was a regular visitor at your house and I should like an explanation of—these." He slapped down on the desk the packet of papers from the safe that Bob had given him.

Mr. Trefold Morton gobbled for a moment, sat down again, then admitted to having financed the club. He denied having any say in, or knowledge of, the way the club was run. He insisted that it had been a speculative investment undertaken from altruistic motives; that he had no thought of profit, merely a laudable desire to provide the youth of Brettenden with a social club that would keep them out of mischief. If his generosity had been abused in any way he, himself, could hardly be blamed.

Delphick made no comment on this, but keeping his eyes on the solicitor, said:

"I should also like a full explanation of the entries in this." He withdrew the black notebook from his pocket and held it in his hand.

Mr. Trefold Morton gazed at it, hypnotised; then of their own volition his hands made a small wringing movement.

Seeing that he had broken, that he had, finally, come apart at the seams, Delphick cautioned him and picked up the telephone.

"Get me Chief Inspector Brinton at Ashford, please... . Chris? ... The holding charge will be embezzlement and breach of trust... . Yes. Incidentally, from something we've learned since, I think I can tell you the meaning of Miss Seeton's last words." From the corner of his vision, he noted the solicitor flinch. "She was trying to tell us that 'chummy' of our recent conversation was Lebel... . Right... . And to you... . Good night."

# Chapter 12

"Nasty piece of work, wasn't he, sir?" observed Bob as he and his superior set out for Plummergen the next morning.

"Yes," agreed Delphick, "I'm bound to admit that I find myself in entire sympathy with his housekeeper; I never could take to him, not from the first. How she stuck him for nearly twelve years …"

They had stuck him until after three o'clock that morning, when Mr. Trefold Morton had been removed to a cell for what was left of the night.

Faced with the proof of his frauds, on that particular subject the solicitor had whined quite freely, the recurring theme of his chant being sorrow for himself. His attitude was that, except in the case of the nephew from Scotland of whose existence he had been unaware, none of the clients concerned had either near relatives or friends to inherit. In consequence the properties would have gone to charities or to the Crown and he felt, he felt strongly, that considering his position, he had as much right, indeed more right, to the money than they. That he had beggared his clients whilst they were still alive, he admitted to be true, but what else, he asked tearfully, could he have done? If he had waited until their deaths, it would have been too late to take action.

When Delphick, restraining anger, pointed out that certainly in the case of Miss Worlingham and probably in that of Mr. Foremason, he had not only robbed people who had trusted him but had also been directly responsible for their deaths, Mr. Trefold Morton shrugged. If people were too stupid or too indifferent to look after their own affairs, to look after themselves, what else could they expect?

On the question of drugs, they could wring no admission from him. He denied ever having seen the curious shaped bottle before, declaring that if it had been found at his office premises, it had either been planted, or else that it must belong to one of his staff and Delphick was in no position to press the matter further until an analysis had been made of the contents. The story of Miss Hant and her bottle Mr. Trefold Morton dismissed as the ravings of an unbalanced mind. He insisted that the pills that he had given to Miss Seeton out of kindness, purely out of kindness, were some proprietary brand of headache cure whose name he had forgotten and, as Mrs. Venning had destroyed the bottle in question, and Miss Seeton was not there to testify, there the matter had to be left.

When Mr. Trefold Morton had been taken away, the Duty Sergeant had produced tea and camp beds. Superintendent Delphick had settled to sleep in reasonable comfort, while Sergeant Ranger, for whom the camp bed was far too short, had settled in unreasonable discomfort on the floor.

Bob slowed the car. "Do you mind if we stop here for a moment, sir? There's something I want to get."

"Go ahead."

Delphick watched Bob enter a florist's shop, then settled back in his seat to plan his next moves. As usual, the wretched Lebel had disappeared into thin air. There must be good organisation behind him. Still that was only to be expected. Drugs meant big money. Big money meant big resources. Were Lebel's repeated attacks upon Miss Seeton in the nature of a personal vendetta, or on orders from above? It was a profitless speculation, Delphick decided. Whatever the reason, Lebel seemed determined to continue having a go which was what chiefly concerned the police. It would have been pleasant to have nailed Trefold Morton for his part in last night's attempt, but it didn't look as if there was going to be a chance of proving it. Thank the Lord that, owing to the solicitor's confession over the embezzlement, he himself hadn't been needed at the Magistrate's Court this morning. Chris Brinton had arranged for someone else to present the police case and to ask for remand without bail, with the possibility of further charges. The further charges part didn't look too promising. Without a great deal more than they'd got, they'd never get a drugs charge to stick. Anyway, he'd passed all his gen on to Narcotics. Maybe they'd come up with something. Their best chance might be Miss Hant. There was the possibility that Trefold Morton had been slipping her doses of the hard stuff when he visited her in the nursing-home. If so, she might blow the gaff on him when her supplies were cut off. He must have a word with Dr. Knight. At worst the solicitor should cop a good stretch for embezzlement. So that was one unpleasing specimen knocked out of the ring, who would never in any real sense get off the floor again. Dealing with drug traffickers was like dealing with an ants' nest. You trod on a few unimportant workers, but you never seemed to get to the heart of the next. To the inner ring of workers. Let alone the queen. Or was it—a king? Anyway, the leader. Boiling water was good for ants. He watched himself striding down the labyrinthine corridors of an ants' nest, with a kettle in his hand, demanding "Take me to your Leader". The kettle tipped, spilling boiling oil. Now, that was an idea. If he could use … boiling oil … that should prove … it should definitely prove … something.

He jerked awake as Bob returned carrying an enormous sheaf of flowers and the largest box of chocolates that Delphick had ever seen. Bob laid his purchases on the back seat, got in and started the car.

"I thought as we were calling at the nursing-home, sir—well, I thought …"

"And a very nice thought, too, Bob. Provided she's there."

Bob was confident. "Oh, she will be, sir."

Delphick was less confident. "I wish I could feel as sure. She's got amazing powers of recuperation. After a good night's sleep, she's just as likely to be skipping round with her umbrella, stirring up mayhem in all directions. Speaking for myself, for a nice twelve-hour kip, I wouldn't need to be given an injection—just the chance."

At the nursing-home, Bob got out and collected his offerings from the back of the car. Delphick remained in his seat.

"I'll stay put, Bob, till you've checked whether Miss Seeton is really here."

"Right, sir."

Bob pushed past the swing doors and looked round the empty hall. Anne Knight, in nurse's uniform, came quickly through a door on his right.

"I saw your car from the window. I'm afraid you're too late. Miss Seeton's gone. She didn't seem any the worse for last night and as soon as she'd had her breakfast, she said she really couldn't laze about in bed any longer. And off she went." Bob gazed at her dumbly and Anne realised what he was carrying. She smiled. He looked so like a love-sick suitor. What a shame Miss Seeton hadn't been there to receive him. "Oh, what a charming thought. How sweet of you. I know she'll love them. If you take them along to her cottage, I think you'll find her there."

Bob advanced upon her, his face crimsoning, and thrust his purchases into her arms.

"For you," he said. He turned and walked out.

Mrs. Knight, coming downstairs, found her daughter sitting on the bottom step, clutching what appeared to be half the garden wrapped in paper and a small crate of chocolates.

"Darling. Have you got an admirer?"

Anne raised a tear-stained, smiling face. "Have I, Mummy? I'm not sure. He's only spoken two words since I met him."

"What were they?"

" 'For you!' "

"Then you have," decided her mother. "But I shouldn't cry about it. It's good for the flowers, but ruination to chocolates. Come along."

She helped her daughter cart the booty into the sitting-room.

* * *

"Miss Seeton's left, sir. They say she's gone home."

"Oh." Delphick refrained from comment on Bob's flushed face and wooden expression, forbore to glance towards the back seat, even managed not to smile. "I see. Then we'd better get along there. Carry on, Sergeant."

"A fight to the death. Both took up their swords.

"Wham. Bang. Bang. Whang. Wham. ScrrOUNCH.

"'Stop. Stop,' cried Jack the Rabbit.

"'Why?' asked Wally Weasel.

"'Because I've broken my sword,' said Jack.

"'That makes mine longer,' said Wally. 'I shall win. Remember it's a fight to the death.'

"'Of course if is,' said Jack. 'But look, my sword's got long jagged splinters. I might hurt you.'

"'Oh!' said Wally.

"'We shall have to call it off,' said Jack.

"'Yes, I see that,' said Wally.

"Jack held out his paw. So did Wally.

"Little Lucy sat on the umpire's knoll and smiled.

"Arm in arm the two enemies walked into the rising sun.

"'I do wish people would look where they're going,' said the sun.

THE END"

She pulled the sheets out of the typewriter, picked up two more and began to insert the carbon. Her mouth twisted. She wouldn't need a carbon of this. At least they wouldn't be able to say she'd failed them. In that respect, anyway, her conscience would be clear. They'd paid her an advance and the

181

book was finished. The story was finished. She put a single sheet of paper into the typewriter, rolled it to the middle and typed:

THE HUTCH THAT JACK BUILT

She sensed a movement, looked up and saw Miss Seeton standing in the doorway. They stared at each other for a long moment. Then:

"If you'll wait one minute while I finish this." She turned back to the typewriter and completed the title page:

by Sonia Venning

She laid the page on top of the completed manuscript, slid the whole into a large stamped envelope addressed to her publishers, and stuck down the flap. Mrs. Venning pushed her chair back, rose and went to the fireplace. She held cold hands to the blaze, but felt no warmth. Without turning her head, she spoke:

"Will you sit down?"

Miss Seeton hesitated, then moved into the room. "I know you won't wish to see me. But I had to come."

"Of course."

Miss Seeton sat on the edge of a chair, her bag and her umbrella in her lap. "I did knock. But there seemed to be no one about. And then I heard the typewriter, so I came through the kitchen and knocked again."

Mrs. Venning's gaze was still on the burning logs. "I'm sorry. I didn't hear you. Mrs. Fratters isn't here. I wanted—I thought it better for her to be out of the house for a day or two. She's staying at her sister's."

Miss Seeton leaned forward. "I didn't mean to interrupt you."

"It doesn't matter."

Miss Seeton tried again. "I know it doesn't help to say I'm sorry. But I am. Most dreadfully, dreadfully sorry."

"That doesn't matter either." Still contemplating the fire, Mrs. Venning straightened and leaned against the beam across the inglenook. "In any case I see no reason why you should be sorry. Quite the reverse. Mrs. Fratters heard the whole story last night from Lady Colveden and the police and told me." Her mouth hardened. "I understand that my daughter and some friend of hers tried to run you down in a car. He then killed my daughter and you were lucky to escape with your life."

"Oh, no. No," breathed Miss Seeton. "It's wicked, wicked. How can they—dare to say such things. I was so afraid that it would all get twisted. That was why I felt I had to come. I know it can't help you now—but it might later. Your daughter knew nothing of what was happening. She didn't suffer." Miss Seeton made a helpless gesture. Then went on: "I feel I should have been able to help. To do something. But when that dreadful boy ran the car into the tree, I slipped and fell into the water. And then it was all so quick. I saw him drag your daughter from the car. But she was quite limp. She couldn't have known. And then he"—she caught her breath and closed her eyes tightly; forced herself to go on—"he killed her. But, believe me, she couldn't have felt—anything. I think I tried to scream. But I don't remember any more." She frowned, uncertain: "Except …"

"Except?"

Miss Seeton made an effort to remember. "Except some man—hitting me on the ground. But I think that was a dream." She looked down. "And that's all."

Mrs. Venning turned away, to move about the room, aimless, restless. When she spoke, her sentences were brief and clipped. "I'm sorry I was so rude to you when you first came …"

"Oh, please."

"I was frightened and worried. And I misunderstood you. I made a mistake." She gave a short laugh. "Just one more of so many bad mistakes."

"But, please," protested Miss Seeton, "you have nothing to apologise for. I knew it was a mistake."

"You knew?"

"Why, yes." Her hands fluttered. "Niobe, you see," she said simply.

Mrs. Venning returned to the fire and sat down. She picked up the poker and, forgetting to use it, sat looking at it in her hand. "Niobe?" she said at last. "So you did know. You did know the whole story."

"No, indeed," Miss Seeton disclaimed. "I knew nothing. It was only afterwards, when I tried to sort out my impressions on paper, to draw you, it came out as Niobe."

The silence that followed was so long that Miss Seeton decided that Mrs. Venning had forgotten her presence. Quite understandable. And very natural, too, that she should wish to be alone. Indeed, she herself would never have dreamed of intruding, only it did seem so important Mrs. Venning should know the truth. Should know that that poor girl hadn't suffered. And had been in no way to blame. It might eventually, if only a little, ease the pain of remembering.

She didn't, of course, want to appear rude, but perhaps if she could just slide out of her chair and steal quietly away. Yes. That would be best. Poor woman. It was quite dreadfully sad. And one felt so useless. But it couldn't be good for her to keep staring at the fire like that without blinking. So bad for the eyes. She was beginning to ease herself out of her chair, when the other spoke. Miss Seeton gave a guilty start and sat back.

"Niobe." Mrs. Venning laughed harshly. "Near enough, I suppose. Though I had only one child and it wasn't vanity that started the trouble. It was fear. All my mistakes have been due to fear. Like most people. David," her voice lingered on the name. For a brief moment the harsh lines in her face softened. She looked young. "David," she repeated, "was earning good money when he was killed in a car smash. We'd spent up to the hilt. The future seemed safe and we'd never thought of saving. Angela was two and I was untrained. Apart from a small insurance policy there was nothing. And I was frightened. Someone I had never met contacted me and offered me a way out. If I would start people on the drug habit—without them even realising what it was they had started—I would be paid so much a head."

Miss Seeton caught her breath.

"Oh, it was put differently. Wrapped up in fine words. But that's what it amounted to. The only person I cared about was gone. Why should I care about others? I agreed. It was easy enough. Be a little gayer than usual at a party and when anybody asked you how you managed it: 'But, *dahling*,' " viciously she parodied the social manner of previous years, " 'haven't you heard? These new pills, too *terribly* divine and happy-making. I'll let you have a bottle.' And I did. If anyone

185

had a headache or was out of sorts: 'But, *dahling*, so sad-making and unnecessary. You *must* try these new pills. Too *madly* herbal and harmless, I believe. But quite *too* miraculous. I'll give you some.' And I did. Each time I unloaded a bottle I was paid, very well paid, and given another one. No pressure was ever put on you to unload unless you wanted to. Or rather, unless you wanted the money. You never had to deal with any case a second time. You merely passed on the name and address of whoever you had given the pills to, and the organisation took over from there. The person in question was watched and when the time was ripe, they would casually meet somebody who could supply them with what they wanted—and stronger. The organisation knew they were safe enough. Even supposing you had second thoughts, you were bound to keep quiet for your own sake. They always chose people who had good social contacts and a certain position to keep up, but needed money."

Miss Seeton shifted uncomfortably in her chair. Really, this was a quite appalling story. And so private. One felt very sorry for poor Mrs. Venning. And, obviously, she believed that her daughter's death was in the nature of a retribution. Well, to be fair, Miss Seeton admitted, she herself though not in the least understanding, had sensed something of the kind. Should one say that one was quite sure that poor Mrs. Venning was in no way to blame—to blame, that is for her daughter's death? Because, in other respects, even allowing for her difficult situation at the time and the temptation, one must confess that one was very much afraid that she was—to blame, that is. Then again, it was all so long ago. Surely it would be better not to dwell on it and, Miss Seeton repressed a sigh, most certainly not to speak of it. What could one say? And how could one tactfully, and without appearing unfeeling, suggest that one must be going? Miss Seeton, having thought herself to a standstill, lost her chance as Mrs. Venning continued:

"I was able to afford to engage my old nurse to help me in the flat and with Angela. One evening, when I went to tell Angela her bedtime story, she was still in her bath, and Mrs. Fratters was teaching her that nursery rhyme she'd taught me as a child: 'Don't care was made to care, Don't care was hung. Don't care was put in the pot And boiled till he was done.' That night I was woken by David's voice repeating over and over and over, 'Don't care was made to care, Don't care was hung'. I didn't go out for a week. Mrs. Fratters did all the shopping and I stayed in the flat, trying to decide what to do. I tried putting the stories I invented for Angela down on paper in book form. I was lucky. They were accepted. And successful. When the second book was taken, I felt safe enough to buy this place. I cut all connection with London and tried to start again. It might have worked, if I hadn't still been afraid. Too afraid to throw away the next bottle of pills. Afraid not to keep it by me as insurance against a rainy day, just in case. I stuck it at the back of a medicine cupboard and after some years I forgot all about it. Last year Angela must have found it. Probably one of the times when I had to stay overnight in London for a session with my publishers. I began to notice that she was very gay, lighthearted—and I was glad. Then too gay, too many ups and downs—and I began to wonder. She was always running around with that awful crowd from the club. I suspected they might be introducing her to drugs, though I knew it couldn't be marijuana—I'd have known. It made me remember that damned bottle and

I decided to throw it out, for safety, then get her to a doctor, in case I was right, and find out what could be done. The bottle was gone. I was afraid to call in a doctor for fear of what might come out, what I might be accused of, above all afraid of Angela finding out what I had done in the past. I never even dared to question her. We never discussed it. I stupidly tried to control or cure her myself, by searching her things, by nagging her about where she went and with whom and why—setting her against me. Knowing all the time that it was I who was responsible. Knowing now that I'm responsible for her death. That was why, when you came waving one of those wretched bottles at me, I thought to begin with you were another poor fool like me. Then I was frightened you were from the police, come to test me in some way, to spy on me. I only realised afterwards, when I had time to think, that you couldn't be. That it was just an idiotic coincidence." For the first time she turned and spoke directly to her visitor. "Where did you get it?"

Miss Seeton was flustered. "That sort of phial thing with the headache tablets? Why, from my solicitor."

"Then leave your solicitor and go to the police. Headache tablets!" She laughed with derision. "The old gags. They never fail. It's too late for Angela. Too late for me. But not too late for you—and others. Go to the police."

"Oh, but the police know," Miss Seeton assured her earnestly. "I told them. Oh, not that they were drugs, of course," she added hastily, "because, naturally, I didn't know. And then I"—remembering how Mrs. Venning had slapped it from her hand—"I didn't actually have the phial with me any more. You're quite sure that they were? Drugs, I mean?"

"Quite sure. That bottle—phial, whatever you like to call it—was designed to be unremarkable, but unmistakable."

"Well, of course," Miss Seeton acknowledged, "I'm bound to say that I don't really like him. I find him rather tiresome. But that a solicitor should ... someone in a position of trust ... Drugs ... Somehow I find that quite shocking." Quite shocked, Miss Seeton stood up.

Mrs. Venning rose. "Well, now that you do know, tell the police."

"Oh, but I couldn't do that," protested Miss Seeton, "without involving you. And I wouldn't dream of doing that. You've quite enough worries of your own."

"You're wrong. I've no worries any more. None. You will involve me in nothing. Tell them everything I've told you. It will probably save trouble." She held out her hand. "Goodbye. And thank you. You've been kind. I apologise for having used you as a confessional."

Miss Seeton took the outstretched hand. "There's nothing I can do?" she asked tentatively. "Nothing I can get? No shopping?"

"No. Nothing, thank you. Wait—yes." She went to the desk and picked up the manuscript for her publishers. "There's this." She handed the envelope to Miss Seeton. "If you're going through the village, perhaps you'd be kind enough to take this to the post office. It will probably," a bitter smile, "save delay."

"With pleasure. But, please don't come out. I can find my own way." At the door, Miss Seeton stopped, worried. "You're sure you'll be all right."

"Quite sure," replied Mrs. Venning. "I've done with fear. I've nothing to be afraid of any more."

People's lives, reflected Miss Seeton. So terribly involved. And so sad. Of course most people would consider her own life humdrum and dull. But at least it wasn't complicated, she decided with satisfaction. Though, whatever Mrs. Venning might say, she did not feel that she could tell the police that dreadful story. After all, what good could it do now? It was all over. And surely that poor woman had been punished enough. The less one discussed, or interfered in, other people's affairs, the better. And with regard to Mr. Trefold Morton—well—that was rather difficult. After all, there was nothing definite. Only her own prejudice. And now something that she'd been told. And one did so dislike gossip. But perhaps if she dropped a hint to the superintendent that she'd been told—without mentioning names, of course ... Didn't the French have a word for it? Ah yes. An ondit ... that he wasn't very satisfactory. The superintendent already seemed interested in Mr. Trefold Morton, so he would probably find out anything there was to find out. If there was anything. Mr. Trefold Morton and the drug traffic disposed of, Miss Seeton entered the post office.

Miss Nuttel and Mrs. Blaine, who were on the point of leaving the same establishment, stopped, smiled, bowed and said "Good morning".

How tiresome. One could not, of course, make a scene in public. One would have to smile and bow in return. Or, at least, nod. Miss Seeton looked straight through the two women, then deliberately turned her back. Oh dear. Now she'd been rude. But, thinking of Mrs. Venning and what those two dreadful women had said, she really could not bring herself to ... oh dear. She crossed to that nice Mr. Stillman and handed him the envelope. As he took it from her to weigh it and check the postage, Miss Seeton found herself loth to relinquish it.

"There's something wrong," she murmured.

"No, nothing wrong," Mr. Stillman assured her cheerfully, "in fact it's overstamped." Miss Seeton gazed at him, unseeing, shook her head, then hurried from the shop. Poor old thing, thought Mr. Stillman, all these goings-on had been too much for her. From what he'd heard, she'd have been better off to stay at Dr. Knight's for a bit.

On The Street, Miss Seeton found herself at a loss. This was ridiculous. She'd go straight home. She turned and walked rapidly in the opposite direction.

"My dear Miss Seeton." Both her hands were caught and held. "How fortunate. I've just been to Dr. Knight's to see you and they told me you'd left already. Remarkable. The human frame is wonderfully elastic. But is it wise. I'm sure my sister would say the same. Rest, the great restorer. And while there I called at The Meadows. I've seldom met Mrs. Venning—not one of my congregation I fear—but, more important, one of my people. A tragic loss. Nothing I could say, but I felt bound to say it. I'm shocked to find that she's away. The house is locked. She won't have heard. What a home-coming. Perhaps my sister will know her address. Poor, silly child. Youth is so reckless. To go bathing late at night. If only I had been there. But I didn't hear until this morning. And then you. To plunge to her rescue as you did, they tell me—a simple act of heroism. An example to us all," declared the Reverend Arthur Treeves. He descended from the heights to shake his head and look severe. "If only some that I could name would follow your example. Other stories are going about. I am disturbed. Perversions of the truth.

191

Malicious lies." Emotion coloured his face and deepened his voice. "Ill-natured gossip is a wickedness that spreads like poison gas. I will not have it. I shall put my foot down and stamp upon it. I shall speak my mind."

Miss Seeton stared blindly at the vicar. Of all the sincere and well-intentioned bumble but one word had penetrated. She pulled her hands away.

"Gas," said Miss Seeton.

She moved quickly round him. She began to run.

# Chapter 13

Miss Seeton was not at her cottage. Representatives from the newspapers were. News of the previous night's events was spreading and the news hawks, who had withdrawn to hover with watchful eyes, were once more swooping to the attack. Martha Bloomer had kept them out of the cottage itself, but she was powerless to prevent them from flocking round the gate, pecking about the front garden and making occasional forays into the main garden at the back. The Battling Brolly was headlines again and it was understandable that editors and reporters alike should wish for some story, preferably based on fact, to follow in smaller print under the main heading. Such accounts as they had gleaned around the village were too libellous to print and too diverse to be anything but patently inaccurate. One piece of good fortune, shared equally between Miss Seeton and Dr. Knight's nursing-home, was that news of her visitation there had not been disclosed.

Superintendent Delphick's and Sergeant Ranger's arrival at Sweetbriars was greeted with enthusiam, but their disappearance into the cottage without comment or statement was not so popular.

Martha had no idea where Miss Seeton was, but as she'd taken clean clothes round to the nursing-home for her the night before she'd probably be back for lunch. As for now, well—she might be shopping or with all this crowd round the cottage she might've gone somewhere.

The superintendent was in a quandary. It was essential that Mrs. Venning should be interviewed as well, but he came to the conclusion that Miss Seeton's whereabouts must take precedence. A few discreet telephone calls having produced no results, Delphick and Bob decided that their only course was to seek information in the village.

At the post office, Mr. Stillman proved helpful. Yes, Miss Seeton had been in. She'd come in with something to post. Actually, he thought she was doing an errand for Mrs. Venning as the envelope was addressed to her publishers. Mrs. Venning's publishers of course. And he knew the name because Mrs. Venning always posted her things here and the envelope was overstamped, as Mrs. Venning often did. Well, now that they came to ask him, Miss Seeton had seemed a bit vague. And was in a bit of a hurry when she left.

The vicar, who happened to be in the shop with his sister, added his quota. Yes, he had met dear Miss Seeton upon The Street; had stopped to have a word—to congratulate her, he could do no less, upon her heroism of last night. Remarkable at her age. And such a tragedy, too. And then, with Mrs. Venning not at home, that made it worse. It was to be hoped that she could be reached in time. But he would put a stop to it. Too much had happened, and a great deal too much had been said. It was his bounden duty ... No, Miss Seeton had said nothing of her intentions. She had seemed—well, preoccupied.

"But what did she do?" demanded Delphick.

"Do?" answered the vicar. He was at a loss. "She didn't do anything. She—just ran."

Miss Treeves was exasperated. "Oh, Arthur, do pull yourself together. Where did she run?"

"Why, home, I suppose," her brother told her. "Really remarkable. Most ladies, after a certain age, trot. But she was running. Running like a girl. Really remarkable."

Delphick restrained himself and spoke as to a child. "You saw Miss Seeton run home?"

"Well, no. Not exactly home," admitted the vicar. "She was going in the other direction." Inspiration came to him. "She was going back to Dr. Knight's, I expect."

"And she didn't speak to you?" asked Delphick.

"No," replied the Reverend Arthur.

"Nonsense," cried Miss Treeves. "Do try to think, Arthur. She must have said something."

Her brother became fussed. "Now don't muddle me, Molly. I don't need to think. I'm perfectly clear about it. I tell you she didn't say anything. At least only one word. And, quite obviously, she was thinking of something else."

"What?" pressed Miss Treeves.

"What?" echoed Bob.

"What word?" urged Delphick.

"Gas," said the vicar.

Outside the post office, Delphick and Bob instinctively looked for their car before remembering that on this occasion they were on foot. They began to run.

Miss Treeves, the vicar, Mr. Stillman and the rest of the customers surged on to The Street to join the crowd of villagers and reporters, grouped outside the shop. All watched the fleeing figures of the two detectives. They started to follow. They began to run.

Bob, with more length to his leg, more breath and less years to his credit than Delphick, won the race. The side door, next to the big wooden gates in the boundary wall of The Meadows, was open. Bob pounded through it, down the path by the garage, rounded the hedge, skidded to a crunching halt by the back door and looked down: broken glass, a broken umbrella and two heads with pink faces lying in the open doorway. He drew a deep breath, choked on the reeking gas fumes, then dragged the two bodies on to the path as Delphick panted into view.

"Leave—you, sir—hospital—quickest," gasped Bob.

Delphick, no breath to waste on words, nodded and, holding his handkerchief to his face, plunged into the kitchen.

Having left his blown superior to throw open all the ground-floor windows and to pass on the news by telephone to Ashford, Bob's re-emergence from the lane, on his way to the nursing-home, with Miss Seeton draped over one shoulder and Mrs. Venning slung over the other, was greeted with cheers by the villagers, shouts of approval from the Pressmen and flashes of light from the photographers.

Dr. Knight, appearing from his surgery at the back of the hall, took one look and sniffed.

"Gas?"

"Yes, sir."

"How long?"

"I don't know, sir."

The doctor stood back from the surgery door. "In here. One on the table. One on the couch. Anne," he called up the stairs, "ask your mother to come down and help me—urgent.

Oxygen. Your probationer's back again—overdressed this time, wearing a couple of women as a stole. Prepare two beds, please."

There was nothing to do but to wait.

Delphick waited at The Meadows. He had rung his chief at the Yard to bring him up to date and to prepare him for the sensation that the newspapers were certain to make of the morning's sequel to the events of the previous night. They had agreed, in view of the wild rumors circulating locally, that as soon as he could get a statement from Miss Seeton, Delphick would be well advised in his turn to give a reasonably full and factual statement to the Press. He had paid a brief visit to the nursing-home to confirm that the two witnesses whom he was anxious to question were once again asleep; although on this occasion he could hardly hold the doctor to blame. Dr. Knight had spared a moment to tell him that Miss Seeton was a 'cert and shouldn't be too long now', adding with enthusiasm that she had already vomited twice, which appeared to please him. Mrs. Venning, the doctor diagnosed as 'only a might'. Provided that she did not relapse, provided that pneumonia did not supervene and provided a host of other technicalities that Delphick failed to understand, 'she might make it. No reaction so far; no retching; not even a contraction'. The doctor had shaken his head in disapproval. 'They'd have to see.'

Delphick had retreated, baffled, to the sitting-room to collect Bob for a search of The Meadows, but Anne Knight's entrance had changed his mind. She had come to explain that one of the staff was with Miss Seeton, that her mother and father were busy with Mrs. Venning and, as there was nothing that she could usefully do at the moment, her mother had sent her down to entertain the detectives. Could she get them coffee or anything? Delphick had picked up his cue. Where Mrs. Knight led, he could surely follow.

"Not for me, thanks. I was just going. No, not you, Sergeant," as Bob moved, "you'd better stay here till Miss Seeton recovers. And let me know as soon as she can talk. I shall be over the way at Mrs. Venning's. I hold you responsible for her. She's not to get loose again till I've seen her. There's no knowing what she might get up to. She's not to go out. If necessary, arrest her, take her umbrella away, anything you like, but keep her here until I arrive."

"Oh, sir, I nearly forgot." Bob reached into his raincoat pocket and withdrew Miss Seeton's umbrella. It was broken. He placed the remains gently on the arm of the sofa, where it lay bedraggled, like a bird with a broken wing. "It was lying near her," Bob went on, "so I stuffed it into my pocket. It—well, it didn't seem right somehow to leave it behind."

The two detectives regarded it in silence. Watching their respectful attitudes, their sombre faces, Anne had the impression that they were mourning the death of an old friend.

Delphick sighed. "I'm sorry about that." He picked up the relic. "I'll ask Miss Seeton, of course, but I doubt she'll want it back. And, if not, I think I should like to keep it as a memento." He moved to the door. "By the way, Sergeant, you might ring Mrs. Bloomer and explain. Otherwise she'll be worrying." Delphick took his leave.

Outside, P.C. Potter had rounded up the local inhabitants, herded them back into the village and sent them about their normal pursuits. Delphick got rid of the reporters by promising to give a Press conference, at The George and Dragon, as soon as he was free. Potter, who had stationed himself at the nursing-home gates in order to prevent any further attempt at unlawful assembly, turned to the superintendent with eagerness.

"Anything further you'd be wanting me to do, sir?"

Delphick gazed at him absently for a moment, then: "Why, yes, constable. If it won't interfere with your other duties, I should be glad if you could help me search The Meadows."

"Yes, sir. Certainly. A pleasure, sir."

"See if we can find any trace of a connection between the girl and Lebel. Any trace of drugs. Anything at all. We shan't, of course, but we have to look. Even if we can only trace the whereabouts of that woman—what's her name—who looks after Mrs. Venning, it would be something." Delphick began to walk down the lane.

P.C. Potter, personal assistant, in person, to a superintendent from Scotland Yard, paced beside him. "Mrs. Fratters, you mean, sir. I'm afraid she's gone off, sir."

Into Delphick's mind, which had wandered ahead of him, intruded a picture of Mrs. Fratters suddenly, inexplicably, having started to decay. He pulled himself together. This lack of sleep was beginning to tell. "Gone off? Where?"

"To her sister's, so she said, sir, when I saw her this morning getting on the Ashford bus. And none too happy about it, too, sir, as I understand it, sir. Not wanting to go. But said that Mrs. Venning had said that she wanted to be alone for a day or two. I suppose you can understand it, sir."

"Yes," agreed Delphick, "I suppose I can."

Bob, waiting at the nursing-home as instructed, put down the telephone and returned to the sitting-room.

"I got on to Mrs. Bloomer," he told Anne, "and she said she'd have something ready whenever Miss Seeton got back. And it wouldn't matter when as it was a cold veal and ham pie." He sounded wistful. "Poor Miss Seeton. I don't suppose she'll be feeling much like food."

Anne handed him a plate of cakes and poured the coffee that she had prepared while he was telephoning. She laughed. "Don't be too sure. I don't think anything Miss Seeton did would surprise me. Remember she's been taking a lot of exercise. And lost her breakfast into the bargain. She ought to have been feeling pretty sorry for herself this morning, but she wasn't. Dad says he's never seen anybody like her for her age. He says she's tough as a boot and can't think how she does it. What exactly did she do, by the way?"

Bob looked puzzled. "Well, we don't really know. She was talking to the vicar and apparently she suddenly said the word 'Gas' and ran off like a scalded cat. But we don't know how she knew." He sat down on the sofa beside Anne and started to eat a cake. "The kitchen window at The Meadows was smashed. That must have been how she broke her umbrella. And then she must have climbed in—or rather dived in; it's only a tiny window—over the kitchen sink, switched off the oven, unlocked the door and dragged Mrs. Venning out. They were both lying in a heap in the doorway when I got there. The place reeked."

"So you just picked them up and brought them to us."

"Well, yes," acknowledged Bob. "We hadn't got the car, you see. I did think of ringing for an ambulance, but it would have wasted time. It seemed quicker really to cart them over and dump them here."

Anne smiled at him. "Which probably saved Mrs. Venning's life."

Bob brooded. "She won't thank me for that."

"Not now, maybe," she conceded. "But if she does win through, she may later. I think if people are meant to die they do and if they're meant to be saved they are and that's all about it."

Bob gazed at her, lost in admiration for this simple, splendid philosophy; this simply splendid girl. Anne grew embarrassed under his steady regard.

"Oh," she said, "how awful. I haven't even thanked you for the flowers and chocolates."

It was Bob's turn for embarrassment. He looked out of the window, eyed the blaze of colour in the beds around the lawn dismally and apologised. "I see now. Stupid of me, I didn't think. Coals to Newcastle."

"Rubbish," she replied. "I've always thought that Newcastle's probably very grateful for the coal. Think of the work it must save them." She eyed the blaze of colour in the vases around the room happily, picked up the box of chocolates and offered: "Have some. They're very good."

Bob put down the empty cake plate, took a chocolate, bit into caramel and was rendered speechless.

Anne gurgled. "I thought you were bringing them for Miss Seeton. You know, I like her. She's a funny little thing and I hardly know her at all, but I like her a lot. I think she's a pet, don't you?"

"M'm'm!" said Bob, fighting to free his teeth.

"Some of them are awful. Take old Miss Hant. For all of me, anyone can take her; she's a horror."

"Doesn't make any difference," mumbled Bob.

"Believe me, it does," she contradicted him, "if you have to cope with them. Miss Hant's been creating half the morning."

Bob, having won his fight, swallowed quickly and burst into speech; it came out louder than he had intended. "It doesn't make any difference," he shouted. He blushed, turned down the volume and continued, "I mean it doesn't make any difference as to how you feel about them. Not always, I mean. I mean you can suddenly see someone and know exactly how you feel about them. Know that's it, I mean. Know that you always will feel like that about them, I mean." He reviewed his exposition and wondered if he had made his meaning clear. The call of duty echoed in his thoughts and he came down to earth. "What was that about Miss Hant?" he asked. "What's wrong with her?"

Anne was disappointed. Bother Miss Hant. Just when the conversation had been going so well. "There's nothing wrong with her—at least nothing more than usual. Apparently she was expecting a visit from her solicitor this morning and was upset because he hasn't been yet."

"And he won't," said Bob.

"Oh, I expect he will," she replied. "As I told her, he's probably busy. He might look in this afternoon, or else tomorrow morning.

"No, he won't," said Bob, "he's in quod."

Anne gasped. "In prison? Mr. Trefold Morton? But he can't be. He's a solicitor."

"That's why." And Bob proceeded to give her a résumé of his and The Oracle's late night final.

Anne was shocked. Impulsively, she put her hand on his arm. "I think it's wicked. You can hardly have had any sleep at all. You must feel awful."

Bob placed his hand over hers. "I feel fine."

"And to think of bringing me flowers and chocolates when you must have been so tired."

"That was easy," Bob told her. "I was thinking of you all the time."

"But …"

He leaned closer. "You know—you must know—how I feel about you."

Anne tried to draw her hand away. She failed. "No, I … Yes, I … But you can't. Oh, you don't understand," she cried in desperation. "Look at me—I'm plain."

He looked; past the trim figure, the neat uniform, to let his eyes linger on her face. "Yes," he agreed.

She turned her head away. "Well—there you are."

Bob addressed the back of her head. "I love you," he said.

Dr. Knight opened the door. He stopped. "I imagine it's compulsive," he observed.

Still holding Anne, Bob leaped to his feet, realised, then hurriedly lowered her to the floor.

The doctor watched them with interest. "Yes, obviously compulsive," he decided. "As you know, Anne, I would be the last to interfere, but I feel it only right that you should be apprised of the facts and be warned."

Anne grinned at him. "What's compulsive, Dad?"

Her father looked severe. "This habit he's got. Picking up women, carrying them about and then putting them down somewhere else. Once could be an impulse. Two—especially two at a time—must be viewed with grave concern. But three—that's compulsion. To the best of my knowledge, it's a completely new symptom and I doubt there's a cure. I'm only speaking for your own good," he told her.

"You will have to give due consideration to the fact that, whatever you may be doing at any particular time, you may be suddenly grabbed off your feet and put down somewhere else in a completely different position. That is ... h'rm." Realising that his flight of fancy had taken him further into the stratosphere than he had intended, the doctor cleared his throat, abandoned the flight and bailed out. He brightened and turned to Bob. "On the other hand, young man, if any time you need a job, let me know. Should we ever be slack, we could always drum up trade by sending you out as a retriever."

Bob stood, huge and hugely embarrassed. His mouth opened in preparation for speech; to explain; to apologise. Inspiration failed him and his mouth closed.

"In view of your very natural anxiety," continued the doctor with glinting enjoyment, "and to forestall those eager questions which I feel sure a natural diffidence, rather than a lapse of memory, is restraining you from asking, I had better give you the latest news of your patients." Bob started: Mrs. Venning, Miss Seeton—he'd forgotten them. "Which was the reason for my interrupting your—um—discussion with my daughter. Mrs. Venning may do, I think; though I suspect a slight heart condition there. No question of an interview, I'm afraid. Even with complete quiet, it'll be touch and go for the next day or two. Miss Seeton, on the other hand, is as bobbish as can be. Extraordinary resilience. Wish I knew her secret. She must be made of India-rubber. You can talk to her any time you like. She wanted to go home, but I've forbidden it. She ought to need rest, even if she doesn't, so I've ordered her to stay in bed."

Behind him, Miss Seeton gave a polite cough. Dr. Knight spun round, blocking the doorway. "Get back to bed, woman, I told you to stay there."

Miss Seeton smiled at him and held out her hand. "Yes, I know, doctor, a most kind suggestion, but I'm quite all right now and I wouldn't dream of troubling you further. The nurse tells me that Mrs. Venning is a little better. Such a relief. So thank you again," she withdrew her hand. "I really do feel that I must go."

# Chapter 14

It was over. Superintendent Delphick felt depressed as he and Sergeant Ranger journeyed back to London by train. The Assize had gone well enough. As for young X, or the Ginger Nut as the papers called him, his dumbness had got him no place: detained during Her Majesty's pleasure, under medical supervision; so he'd be kept locked up until he spoke and if he spoke they'd lock him up for having spoken—which settled his hash. His defending counsel had been doing well and it had looked a bit tricky until Miss Seeton had started complaining about the damage to her hat—trust her to pull a rabbit out of it. From then on, once the laughter had died down and they'd restored order in Court, there'd never been any doubt. The foreman of the jury could hardly wait for the end of the judge's summing up before bouncing to his feet to announce his popular, if unconventional: "There's no need for us to retire, Your Honour, if it's all the same to you. He's guilty of all you said and a sight more besides by our reckoning." Trefold Morton, too, had gone down for a nice stretch for embezzlement. There was still a chance they might catch him out on the drugs as well, but that wasn't his pigeon, it would be up to the Drug Squad. Chris Brinton and the Ashford lot were happy enough: the case had cleared up a few spots of trouble in their manor. But, for himself, there was no blinking the fact that his assignment had been to catch Lebel. And he hadn't. César had run rings around them. The only person who ever seemed to set eyes on him was Miss Seeton herself and she appeared to be fully capable of dealing with him in her own way whenever she did. If César had had another go at her this last week, when they were ready and set up for him ... But obviously Lebel had given his best and chucked it in. She should be safe enough now. And the local bobby'd keep his eyes open. César would pop up somewhere else and they'd pick him up eventually. But meanwhile, for himself, he had to admit—he'd failed. Though they could chalk it up to their credit that if it hadn't been for Bob, Miss Seeton would have been drowned. But after all they weren't in business as lifesavers. No, scrap that—fundamentally, he supposed, that was what they were. Delphick grinned. He was going to frame that broken umbrella of hers and hang it on his office wall as a reminder not to get smug. With Lebel identified it had seemed so easy. From the moment she had poked him in the ribs in Covent Garden and said 'Naughty' or words to that effect, Miss Seeton had laid it on the line for them and they had followed along behind, mopping up this and that as they went, until he'd let himself be hypnotised into believing that she'd produce César and hand him over, neatly trussed and garnished, on a plate. Actually she had produced him—twice—and it was they who had failed to do the trussing. Funny, that trick of hers of being able to see into people's motives and backgrounds, without always fully realising what it was she saw. Or rather drew. They could do with her on the staff at the Yard. A good thing really Narcotics weren't going to try and press charges against Mrs. Venning. One way and another you could say she'd paid her account. In any case, there was only Miss Seeton's report of a conversation; the Venning herself was too ill to make sense and at least they'd learnt a new slant on how people got hooked on drugs—for all the good it would do them.

It was over. Somehow he'd known it would be from the moment Miss Seeton had broken her umbrella. Arm her with a brolly and all hell let loose. But take it away and everything quietened down at once. Pity they hadn't picked up young Caesar, but you couldn't do everything. Caesar wouldn't be any use to his own bosses now that he was marked and Miss Seeton could finger him for the Covent Garden do, and if they thought there was any danger of his talking, they'd probably wipe him out themselves which would save a lot of trouble all round … Anne Knight. It was a beautiful name. Anne … Anne Ranger. Somehow that was even better. More natural. He'd got leave this week-end, she'd promised to come up and they'd have dinner and do a show on Saturday, and on Sunday—he must think of something for Sunday— and … Bob gazed out of the carriage window at his private view of a heart-moving future. It was only just beginning.

It was over evidently. She left the window and sat down as Crabbe's two buses drew up at the garage opposite and spilled out the returning villagers.

"They're back, Eric. Too stupid. I can't think what every-body wanted to go over to Maidstone to the trial for. As if it was a holiday excursion or something."

Miss Nuttel was subdued. "Went to the hearing at Ashford ourselves."

Mrs. Blaine bridled. "After all, we only went because we thought we ought to support somebody who was living here and give them the benefit of the doubt. We should have known better. Anyway, this time there's no doubt at all. We've learnt far more by staying here and only proved how too right we were all along."

Her friend demurred, worried. "Still think we ought to get on to the police, Bunny."

"Nonsense, Eric. They'd only believe her and she'd make fools of them as she always does. It's too obvious to me that she's in league with this young murderer from London and has been all the time and I've always said so. And this afternoon has proved it. Watching him creep into her house like that as soon as everything had quietened down and he thought the village was empty and no one would see. I'll bet he's hiding here waiting for her to come back. She hasn't had a chance before, with the police all over the place. It's all too clear. As soon as she gets back—and trust her to have wangled a police-car to take her and not use the bus like anybody else—she and that boy'll get together and there'll be trouble. You'll see."

Well, it was over and, really, it had not proved as bad as one might have feared. It had been unpleasant, of course, having to give evidence against that young man with the reddish hair, whose name nobody appeared to know and, indeed, his counsel had been almost rude, trying to make out that she and that nice lorry driver had been responsible for damaging his brain—the young man's brain, that was—by leaving him to roll about in the back of his van; but, after all, it hadn't been

209

for very long and, as she had pointed out, she had been in the back of the van, rolling about, for much longer—and with a sack over her head—and it hadn't damaged her brain, only her hat. Actually the whole case was over much quicker than she had expected. The judge—such an understanding-looking man—had made it all so very clear. And then she had imagined that there would have to be a wait while the jury retired, but they hadn't. As the proceedings hadn't taken very long, perhaps they hadn't needed to. So extremely lucky, too, that she wasn't after all called as a witness in Mr. Trefold Morton's trial in the afternoon. Though, of course, it had meant waiting about in case. But, apparently, he had admitted to embezzling other people's money—really, quite shocking for a man in his position. In any event, she didn't see how she could have helped them over embezzlement, even if they had asked her because, quite frankly, it had never occurred to her that he did.

The police car drew up at the gate of Sweetbriars and Miss Seeton, thanking the driver who had jumped out to open the door for her, alighted. He smiled at her, saluted, got back into the car and set off on his return journey to Ashford.

So thoughtful of them to have provided a car for her. Now she came to think of it, she had to admit that she did feel rather tired. Oh dear, should she have tipped the man? It was so difficult to know. He didn't look as if he'd expected it. But then again, in the ordinary way, the less people looked as if they expected a tip, the more they did in fact expect. No, of course, one never tipped police. It was called bribery. Though, from what she'd read, one did in certain countries abroad. And, of course, in America, where the system was probably quite different.

Miss Seeton stood for a moment in happiness looking at her cottage before walking up the short path to unlock her front door.

How nice to be home. To think that there were only two more days before she had to go back to London for the beginning of the new term. How the time had flown. What with one thing and another, she never seemed to have had the chance to get down to learning about gardening as she had meant to do. Though this last week, after that dreadful affair by the pond, had been quite peaceful. Poor Mrs. Venning. Such a relief that she had recovered. And yet, Miss Seeton wondered, would it perhaps have been better if she hadn't? Should one perhaps not have interfered? The trouble was one acted on the spur of the moment, without really thinking of the consequences. Dr. Knight had told her that Mrs. Venning had now had a complete breakdown and that they had flown her out to some sort of nursing-home in Switzerland, to get her away from all the past unhappy associations. And, of course, the air there—so very pure. Good gracious, what was that?

A long, flat parcel lay on the table in the passage. Miss Seeton picked it up.

Now, who could have … ? She didn't remember having ordered anything. Beautifully wrapped. It must be from a shop. And with that clever sticky tape to hold it down that was so quick and easy to do and so quite—she wrestled with it—impossible to undo.

Eventually there emerged from the torn brown paper a narrow white cardboard box. Inside, wedged into place with tissue paper, gleamed under its polythene sheath a slim black silk umbrella with a card tied to its yellow metal handle.

But who could have sent her this?

Miss Seeton pulled the handle towards her in order to read the card. From behind her there came a click.

What? She turned. Oh, yes, of course, she'd knocked the cupboard door shut. How stupid. One forgot how narrow the passage was. She looked at the umbrella's ferrule—no, she hadn't damaged it. Martha had warned her to keep that door bolted because the latch was inclined to slip and one could get a nasty bang in the dark. But, surely—yes, surely—she had bolted it. This morning before she left, after putting the hoover away. Well, obviously she hadn't. Because Martha had gone to Maidstone this afternoon and nobody else would have been here. And, besides, both the front and back doors had been locked. How very careless, she might easily have been hurt.

Miss Seeton shot the bolt. Prudently she moved into the sitting-room to read the card.

'Superintendent Alan Delphick, C.I.D. New Scotland Yard.' But why?

Miss Seeton turned the card over; on the back there was a handwritten note.

'In reparation for your loss in the course of duty. A.D.' She felt quite overwhelmed. Really, how very kind. And to realise that one preferred a crook handle, so much more practical, to a strap whose stitching was always giving way.

Miss Seeton noticed a mark on the handle; looked closer.

But good gracious, it wasn't metal at all. It was gold.

Proudly, Miss Seeton placed her new umbrella in one of the clips on the passage wall above the drip-tray.

It was a little late for tea now. And she was tired. No, she would go upstairs and do her exercises. It would be a pity to miss them as they did seem to be doing her a great deal of good. And then she would fetch her tray, take it up and treat herself to supper in bed.

The bell of the egg-timer rang and Miss Seeton, in the corner of her bedroom, lowered her feet to the floor.

She was improving. She was coming down much more slowly now. Though her feet did seem to have landed with rather a thud. She remained huddled on the floor for a moment with her head down, taking deep, regular breaths. Surely ... Perhaps it hadn't been her feet. Yes, surely someone was knocking downstairs. She caught up her dressing-gown, hurried into the front bedroom and looked out of the window. No—there was no one there. Either she must have been mistaken, or it must have been at some other house.

Seven ... eight ... nine ... She stopped counting her breaths in order to listen. There was quite definitely someone knocking. And it was here—she could feel the vibration. She pulled her feet off her thighs, straightened her legs, got up quickly and staggered. Oh dear, of course one should take one's time—a little massage and then bend forward—before trying to walk. She put on her dressing-gown again and went downstairs.

There was no one at the front door. She hesitated. Two more taps sounded, fainter than the previous ones. It was probably a branch against a window, decided Miss Seeton. She repaired to the kitchen.

She'd collect her supper-tray and take it up now that she was down. After all there was only one exercise that she hadn't completed, and really she didn't feel that she could start again.

At the foot of the stairs, she heard a slithering sound and then a bump against the cupboard door. She stooped to lower the tray.

Oh dear. Probably the hoover. She'd been in a hurry this morning and she hadn't been sure at the time that she'd balanced it correctly on that box. She must have a proper clear-out of that cupboard and make more room. But—no. Not tonight. She was too tired. Miss Seeton straightened and began to mount the stairs. Martha and she could sort it out tomorrow. Whatever it was that had fallen down in there could be picked up in the morning.

# Preview

It's practically a Royal Marriage! The highly eligible son of Miss Seeton's old friends Sir George and Lady Colveden has wed the daughter of a French count.

Miss Seeton lends her talents to the village scheme to create a quilted 'Bayeux Tapestry' for Nigel and his bride. But her intuitive sketches reveal a startlingly different perspective—involving buried Nazi secrets, and links to a murdered diplomat and a South American dictator …

Serene amidst every kind of skulduggery, this eccentric English spinster steps in where Scotland Yard stumbles, armed with nothing more than her sketchpad and umbrella!

The new Miss Seeton mystery

COMING SOON!

# About the Miss Seeton series

Retired art teacher Miss Seeton steps in where Scotland Yard stumbles. Armed with only her sketch pad and umbrella, she is every inch an eccentric English spinster and at every turn the most lovable and unlikely master of detection.

## Further titles in the series—

# About the author

**Heron Carvic** was an actor and writer, most recognisable today for his voice portrayal of the character Gandalf in the first BBC Radio broadcast version of *The Hobbit*, and appearances in several television productions, including early series of *The Avengers* and *Dr Who*.

Born Geoffrey Richard William Harris in 1913, he held several early jobs including as an interior designer and florist, before developing a successful dramatic career and his public persona of Heron Carvic. He only started writing the Miss Seeton novels in the 1960s, after using her in a short story.

Heron Carvic died in a car accident in Kent in 1980.

# Note from the Publisher

While he was alive, series creator Heron Carvic had tremendous fun imagining Emily Seeton and the supporting cast of characters.

In an enjoyable 1977 essay Carvic recalled how, after having first used her in three short stories, "Miss Seeton upped and demanded a book"—and that if "she wanted to satirize detective novels in general and elderly lady detectives in particular, he would let her have her head ..."

You can now **read one of those first Miss Seeton short stories** and **Heron Carvic's essay in full**, as well as receive updates on further releases in the series, by signing up at http://farragobooks.com/miss-seeton-signup